STILL WATER RUNS DEEP

Appalachian Short Stories

Jim Hays & Rob Williams
Sketches by Ann Adams Hays

Published by Appalachian Imprints
P.O. Box 337
Berea, Kentucky 40403

Library of Congress Catalog Card Number 95-083669

ISBN # 0-935680-65-9

Original art work by Ann Adams Hays.

Ann Adams Hays, a native of Berea, Kentucky, is a family practice physician at the University of Kentucky Student Health Service. She is married to Lon Hays, brother of the author. They have three children; Lon Stuart, Karolyn and Kathryn.

Cover photograph by Warren Brunner.

The cover photograph was taken in 1977 of Elwood and Martha Ellen Lainhart Hisel while on the porch of their home near Hisel, Kentucky. They had just finished planting potatoes.

CONTENTS

THE LITTLE TED STORIES BY ROB WILLIAMS

THE JOHN L. STORIES BY JIM HAYS

For

Lon Stuart

Karolyn, Kathryn

and

Shelby

IMPRESSIONS

An imprint in the mind; a picture painted to rule the soul.

Lines drawn on the ground by a mule and a bottom plow.

The tracks of a fat ol' possum in a sandy road.

A boy's first squirrel.

The toothless smile of a young child.

A mothers love.

Small things that make a difference; the difference in success and failure.

Lessons taught by actions, not words.

Kindness given to a child; words filled with encouragement.

Enjoyment of a gift given. Enjoyment of a gift received.

Advice screened by the test of time.

A rock pile orphaned by a field.

A pile of weathered barn siding being detained only briefly before returning to the earth.

Briars claiming a field, waiting on trees for reinforcement.

A graveyard giving way to a thicket; stones returned to their natural order.

Ginseng berries ripe and red.

The smell of honeysuckle and fresh cut hay.

A collar that wore out three mules.

A house long outlived by a chimney.

A hole in the ground that used to be a well.

A spring left to run wild.

A set of discs setting in the woods; a testament to battles won but the war lost.

A rock pile orphaned by a field.

Lessons taught by actions, not words

Workin' to eat; eatin' to work.

A rail fence creeping slowly back into the ground.

A rock fence trying to hold its ground from the escaping field within.

The finished product of lesson well taught.

Solemn faces
Deep cut lines
Smiles of the weary transcend time

Strong are the hands
roughened and worn
Testament to the tired and torn.

Overall clad
cotton cap
leather boots
A chin striped with tobacco juice.

Bent by the wind
Tanned by the sun
Toils are plenty
Pay days none.

BAD BILLY PEARSON

When I was a growin' up, Bad Billy Pearson came to pay Uncle John a visit. Billy was a blowin' about how rough a customer he was. Uncle John looked him dead in the eye, opened the drawer of his big roll top desk and took in his hand five .45 cartridges and said, "with these five cartridges I've killed two men, a screech owl and big yeller dog."

You might as well have hit Billy in the face with a flat iron.

Later on, I got to thinkin'; two men, a screech owl and a big yeller dog only adds up to four, not that I'm much on figgerin' numbers.

Maybe Uncle John wasn't much at figgerin' either or maybe Billy knew something I didn't.

ROUNDHEAD JIM MARLOWE

One day I asked Ted who he thought was the baddest man around back in the old days. I had heard Ted's stories about bad men for as long as I could remember and he never failed to tell me that the graveyard was full of 'em. Ted sat down on the wooden bench on his front porch and this is what he told me.

A lot of men talk bad stuff. But most of 'em 're like a bigmouth hound; all bark and no bite. The quiet ones 're the ones you gotta watch. They'll slip up and have ye by the leg before ye know it.

John Willis Cook was the nervyest man we had in these parts. He said what he meant and meant what he said. I grew up in under his feet so I had no fear of him. You couldn't drag most of the bad men to his doorstep.

Now John Willis; we called him Uncle John, was a watchmaker and a gunsmith; the only one in this country. So if you had watch or gun trouble, he was the man to see. He said he picked up watch work in the penitentiary when he was a young man.

You see, years ago times was hard. Most people 'round here made corn likker to get by. Uncle John and Roundhead Jim Marlow had a still under a cliff in the head of the Watkins Holler where the Greasy Tate bunch gets water from now.

Anyway, ol' Roundhead was one of them fellers always a tellin' what he was gonna do to somebody. Uncle John partnered up with him 'cause they was cousins on his mommy's side. They was a makin' likker and doin' right well 'til Roundhead got greedy. Don Pierce was sheriff then and he was crookeder than a dog's hind leg. Him and Roundhead made a plan to catch Uncle John, confiscate his whiskey and sell it. They figgered to turn Uncle John over to the revenuers from Frankfort and while he was locked up,

Roundhead would run the still.

Shore e-nuff, late one evenin' during a hard wind, Don Pierce slipped up on Uncle John while Roundhead was makin' a run. Caught by surprise, Uncle John couldn't get away. The revenuers took him off to do eighteen months in the big jail.

Being a loudmouth, ol' Roundhead got to braggin' 'bout how he had Don Pierce in his shirt pocket. Word got back to Uncle John about this and he was a fumin'. He sent word to Roundhead, "if ye ever speak to me again, I'll kill ye."

A couple of years went by before Uncle John came back to the county. One day he walked in the door of the general store at the Gap. There set Roundhead, big as ye please, tellin' lies and spittin' baccer juice on the big potbellied stove.

My daddy had just walked in as Uncle John made his way by the counter. He said people was a leavin' right and left 'cause they knowed trouble was a brewin'.

"Glad to see ye back in town, Cousin John," he said.

At that very moment , Uncle John pulled out a big .45 from his hip and shot Roundhead right in the mouth.

From that day on, they said Uncle John "said what he meant and meant what he said."

When they took Uncle John to court he pled his own case. He claimed Roundhead brought it on hisself, "cause I said what I meant; meant what I said. If the fool had of kept his mouth shut he wouldn't be fertilizin' the honeysuckles up on the hill today. What good is a man that don't mean what he says?"

The jury must of took to heart what John said. Bugeye Huey Marcum was the foreman. When the judge asked for the verdict, Bugeye made this reply. "Roundhead was a loudmouth, overbearin', doublecrossin' liar, not doing anybody any good. Least now he's a fertilizin' the honeysuckles up on the hill"

The judge said Uncle John was justified in his actions by relieving the community of a menace and I don't reckon anybody bothered Uncle John for the rest of his days.

THE PEDDLER'S HOLE

It was early in the spring when me and my huntin' buddy, Little Ted, was sittin' up on a high cliff above Rock Lick Creek. Ted never did run out of stories and I never cease to wonder how his head had room for all of them. Seems like he knew a little something about most ever'where and ever'thing, at least around Rock Lick anyway. We'd set there a while watchin' a hawk sail on the warm wind comin' down the valley. The trees hadn't leafed out yet and I could see things that I'd never took note of before.

I wondered how long it had took a little stream of water like Rock Lick to carve out a deep holler like the one we sat above.

"See that clift across the way there," said Little Ted pointing to a wall of rock that rose two hundred feet or more out of a flat by the creek. "They's a grave back in that woods on top of that flat."

"Whose is it?" I asked.

"Eli Clark. He's the one that gave the Peddlers Hole its name."

"The Peddler's Hole?"

"Yep, the Peddler's Hole. If you'll look down there to your left you can see it. It looks like a washout at the bend of the creek, but it's not. People always said it didn't have no bottom. Mommy said that granddaddy sunk a rock with a years worth of twine and it never hit the bottom (You see, back then twine was a valuable commodity; people would horde it up to use on the farm.) Yep, legend has it that many a dead mans soul lingers round that hole of water."

"Why's that, Ted?'

"Well, I'll tell ye. You see, Eli Clark and his tribe lived on that long bench around from the Short Holler." Ted pointed to a flat down on the creek below the cliff across from us. "About thirty yards from that big poplar yonder set Eli's house; a two pen it was. Burnt down when I was a boy. He was a deceitful man and they said he was so tight he'd steal the nickels off a dead mans eyes. He'd insure his baby childern; then smother 'em with a piller to collect the insur'nce money. I know about him very well because he was married to my mommy's Aunt Gracie. When they was homesteadin' out in Oklahoma, he got tard of her gripin' about the flat land out there; divorced her; and sent her home. You see, Aunt Gracie couldn't read, so he tagged her like a piece of baggage and sent her to B'rear on the train, but that's a whole differ'nt story."

"Now, years ago, peddlers would come down Rock Lick sellin' ever'thing from snake oil to women's bloomers. Most was lowly men that would hornswoggle a widder woman out of her false teeth. After a while, people got to seein' that the peddlers didn't make it on farther than Eli's. Aunt Mandy always said he'd lure 'em out to the barn fer a drank of corn likker then whack 'em on the head with a broad ax. At night when nobody could see, he'd throw their bodies in that hole o' water with no bottom."

"The first 'uns to figger out what he was a doin' was the turkles. They'd swim from up and down the creek to get in on the free meal that Eli was providin'."

"In his last days, Eli was old and feeble but still mean as the devil even when he took to his death bed. Neighbors had come down the creek to comfort his new wife (a well thought of woman) while ol' Eli was preparin' to meet the Lord. Mommy, Aunt Mandy and Pap was there when it happened."

"Eli screamed, don't let 'em get me! Don't let 'em get me!"

"Mommy said he had fear in his eye. All the folks figgered he was talkin' about the devil."

"By this time Preacher Cap McFarthing had made it to his side. Confess your sins to the Lord, Preacher Cap said."

"The Lord and the devil ain't my worries, Cap. Just don't let them damned ole snappers get me 'fore I die."

"Pap said that him and the other menfolk had made their way up to the porch to have a chaw when they heard a commotion out in the yard. They could see by the light of the lantern that them old snappers was a makin' their way up the bank of the creek and was headed for the house. For the next half hour or so, the menfolk had to pack the turkles to the creek whilest Eli gave up the ghost."

"Eli's woman wouldn't let him be buried on the creek for fear the turkles would dig him up and that's why he's buried way up there on the mountain."

I pondered Ted's story for a while wondering if it really happened. Maybe so. Maybe not. It didn't matter. I guess a man had to have some reason to be buried away from everybody else. Maybe the real truth of Eli Clark's sins would never be known. The hawk sailed out of sight and as we turned to leave I knew that somewhere in the lengthening shadows above the Short Hollow rested Eli Clark under being a blank, tilted gray stone that would eventually fall and be covered with brown chestnut oak leaves. Yes, eventually the only remnant of his existence would be in the stories of Ted and others who would keep this place alive in my mind forever.

JIM

The summer of '31, 'member it like yesterday. Corn got up knee high and dried up. I'll tell you, Longshanks, it was the driest time on earth. Drier than a popcorn fart, it was. Pap figgered we'd better head for greener pastures. Loaded up ever'thing we owned on Bill Sparks coal truck and headed down below!

Grandpap "doll head" Carpenter had already been at Panola fur 'bout a year. He'd just about convinced Mommy it was the promised land compared to the rocky hillside on the creek. Pap, being a mule skinner and blacksmith, would be turning work away at the dusty little crossroads depot call Panola or at least that's what grandpap told us.

J.B. Wilson was one of the two storekeepers at Panola. Like most of the sharecroppers, we run a yearly bill at the store. Now, Jim Davis and his family was the first black people that I ever knowed, and like us, they had an account at the store. The Davises were fine people, they was. Had six young'uns and any one of 'em would give you the shirt right off his back.

Me and Pap was at J.B.'s late one fall evenin' when Jim come in to settle up for the year. J.B. got out the big ledger book and told Jim what he owed. Jim paid up with money he'd earned loadin' tanbark folks had brought down from the hills.

After they'd settled up, ol' Jim stood there for a minute with a bumfuzzled look on this face.

"What's wrong, Jim?" J.B. asked.

"Well, Mr. Wilson, I'd like a receipt.

"Jim, don't you trust me?"

"No sir, it's not that, but one of these days this ol' world gonna come to pass on and I'm gonna see Saint Peter. He gonna say, Jim Davis, did you pay J.B. Wilson what you owed him? Then sir, I'll have to hunt all over hell to git that receipt."

J.B. just laughed and wrote out Jim his receipt."Nice doin' bizness with you, Mr. Wilson," he said as he turned and walked out the door.

Yessir, Longshanks, Jim Davis was nobody's fool. Nobody's.

PUNKIN WEATHER

It was the first dark night in October and me and Little Ted had set off a coon huntin'. It was a brisk night; cold and clear. Punkin weather was what Ted called it.

Ted's ol' Walker Hound, Latch, was the first to strike. It wasn't long before my cur pup, Chainsaw, got in on the race. As the dogs cold-trailed, I was waitin' for a story to start brewin' and shore nuff it did.

"Longshanks," he said, punkin weather always 'minds me of my great-grandmammy Mary Lize."

"Why's that?" I asked.

"Contrary to what most folks believe, dark nights is for witches and haints. Witches like to go visitin' on dark nights and that's how it started with my ol' granny Mary Lize."

It was a dark night when Aunt Sookie visited grandmammy's house a lookin' to stay over. Sookie took a likin' to a big brooch pin granny wore on her shawl. She reckoned that granny ort to let her have that pin. Grandmammy said it was her Eastern Star pin and she wasn't about to part with it.

"Deny me, Mary Lize," warned Sookie, "and bad luck is shore to befall ye." And soon it did.

Next morning when grandmammy got up to cook breakfast, Sookie was gone, but it didn't take long for her spell to hit. As Grandmammy was goin' to the barn to milk, she saw this strange little rabbit at the edge of the garden. Grandmammy was a kind soul, you see. She went to shoo the rabbit with her apron, when a sharp pain hit her in the back. The little rabbit just set there chewin' it's cud, like it was enjoyin' seein' Grandmammy bending over in pain.

Grandmammy seed that rabbit on different occasions that week and ever' time her back got a little worse. To beat it all, the rabbit would just set there an grin like a mule eatin' saw briars. Finally Grandmammy had to take her bed. Her and Grandpap both suspected Sookie Ann had put on a spell.

Grandpap Ab finally decided he'd go see Aunt Sookie and put a stop to the terrible sufferin' Grandmammy was goin' through. He went up to Sookie's cabin just above the forks of the creek. "Sookie Ann," he said, "I know it's you comin' to the house as a rabbit and causin' Mary Lize this sufferin' and if it don't stop I'll put a hurtin' on you."

For about a week, ever'thing went alright, but it weren't long before the rabbit started showing up again and Grandmammy started a hurtin'. Knowin' that the rabbit always met Grandmammy on the way to the barn, one mornin' Grandpap got up two hours afore daylight and crawled into the loft of the barn with his cap and ball pistol. `Bout daylight, Grandmammy was a walkin' to the barn to milk when the rabbit hopped out of the weeds beside her. Afore Grandmammy could reach for her back, Grandpap capped one off. The rabbit went head over heels and Grandmammy throwed the bucket clear acrost the garden. Grandpap come out of the barn like his overhalls was afire aimin' to put an end to the rabbit. But not hide nor hair could he find 'till he met the path headin' toward the forks of the creek. On a little chestnut pole that had fell acrost the path he fount blood and hair.

Another week passed and he'd seen neither the rabbit nor Aunt Sookie. Pap decided to head toward the forks just to see if'n he'd put an end to ol' Sook. When he got to her door he hollered.

She said, "come on in Ab. I ain't able to come to the door."

Pap knowed right then the rabbit was Sookie. He stepped through the door of the cabin and there laid Sookie all covered up a peepin' through the big iron bedstead.

"What's ailin' Aunt Sookie?" he said.

"I fell a goin' to the spring an jobbed a big ol' stob plum through the calf of my leg." She pulled back the cover and showed him the leg all bound up with white rags and coal oil.

"Sookie," he said serous as a heart attack, "if'n that little rabbit shows up in my garden again, they won't be enough white rags and coal oil on this creek to stop up the hole between your eyes." And that was the end of the witchin' problem for Grandmammy Mary Lize.

"Remember Longshanks, when you hear screech owls a hollerin' durin' pumpkin weather a witch could come a callin'.

THE GOLD TOOTH

The summer of '34; 'member it like it was yesterday. It was hard times at Panola. Pap figgered it was time to load up our belongings and head back to the creek where we had come from.

Our cabin on the creek at the head of the Short Hollow had lost its roof during the heavy snow in '32 so we moved in the old Curt Brock cabin up from the forks of the creek. Mommy didn't like the idea of moving there since they had been so much meanness happen on ever' bench below the pourover, which was the waterfall in the creek just below the Curt place.

Pap said that all that meanness had went to rest with the dead and it was either live at the Curt place or live under a ledge - at least 'til we could get a roof on the Short Hollow cabin.

The Curt Brock bunch was mean 'uns, raw-boned, near seven foot tall and stronger than a loggers steer. Curt's boy, Russ, had killed his brother, Hiram, with a broad ax and chopped him across the middle like stove wood. Before Hiram died, he drawed his 32-20 and shot Russ in the back. They laid there and bled out together, no doubt a cussin' each other to the last breath.

Ol' Curt, well, he just disappeared. It was said that him and his boy, Nath, was sweet on the same gal. Some said he was tired of the meanness and headed for Oklahoma to homestead for the rest of his days. Others was a figgerin' he took a trip to the bottom of the peddler's hole wearin' a nice pair of rock shoes.

Mommy set right off a straightenin' up the place. She had me and my little brother, Harve, working like dogs a splittin' boards out in the chipyard. Mommy was real particular about her floors. I guess 'cause she was raised in a two-pen that didn't have any. We had ever'thing in the old house a lookin' purty good, at least to me. Mommy kept frettin' 'bout the broke hearth stone, so me, pap and Harve took the mules and a sled down to the creek to see if'n we could find her a better one. It took some doing but we drug, prized and skidded' til we got a big rock loaded on the sled. Pap laid the plow lines to the old mule and she dug in toward the house.

While pap went to borrow a rock hammer from Willie Harrison, me and Harve started a prizin' the big hearth stone out of the house. We wriggled and prized and prized and wriggled. Finally Harve came up with a good idea and since mommy was gone to pick berries, I figgered we'd give 'er a try. We'd wedge the big half of the rock up, pour a good coat of bacon grease on the floor, chain the rock to the mule and skid 'er right out the front door. I'd work the mule and Harve would grease the floor. That Harve was a good 'un when it came to figgerin' things. (He retired up in Dayton from a sheet metal machine job at a airplane factory.) So here we went. The mule drug that big rock right out the front door slick as could be.

I hadn't even unhitched the mule when Harve came a screamin' ever breath. He run four laps around the house like somebody had set fire to him. "A skull, a skull with a big gold tooth," Harve yelled.

Me and pap run to the house and shore nuff, there it was. Where the hearth stone had been was a skull with a gold tooth.

"We've fount him, son," said pap.

"Fount who?" I asked.

"Old Curt Brock!"

Pap sent Harve up the creek to get Uncle Ty, Willie Harrison, the deputy sheriff, and whoever else he could find. When they all got there and got the bones all dug up, Willie said it was shore to be Curt Brock. Nobody on that creek was that big or has been since. But, most of all, it was that gold tooth. Ever'body that knowed him had heard him brag about robbin' this Italian stone cutter of his gold pieces and having his tooth fixed after he got out of the big jail in Frankfort.

As Uncle Ty and Willie were fillin' up coffee sack (it took almost two) with bones, Harve went to pointin' at a rib bone. "Looky there at that bullet, pap!" There lodged in a rib bone was the bullet that killed Curt. Uncle Ty reckoned it was a .45 long Colt like Nath packed. Pap put it in a jar with the buttons and buckles.

Sunday of that week, we buried Curt. Grandpa Ab fixed him a nice pine box. Mommy and Mandy McFarthing fixed the inside with gingham and quilt battin'. We buried him high on the hill under the red oak beside the rest of his boys.

Mommy said she wasn't a livin' in a house what had had a man buried in it and ever'body on the creek helped to get a roof on the Short Hollow cabin in record time.

I was down on the creek not long ago and the chimney to the Curt place is still standing. Not far away is half of a hearth stone; a tribute to Curt.

THE IRON KETTLE

The pick-up bumped off the Old State Road and down the dirt driveway to Aunt Minnie's house. John L. had promised Minnie that he would mail some packages for her, so he had left his house early this morning on his way to school. It seemed that he'd been behind every car on Lishes Branch, not to mention the school bus. The turn into Minnie's driveway was real sharp and John L. had to go slow in order to make the turn before he drove on down to the flat place in front of the house, where company parked. Aunt Minnie had never owned a car; and her husband who had died some forty years before hadn't had one either, so John L. figured that the entrance had been designed for a buggy or wagon and respected its narrow uniqueness as such. Actually, Minnie wasn't John L.'s aunt, but everybody called her aunt, as a title of respect.

By the time John L. had crossed the wide planked front porch, Minnie was headed to the bedroom to get her packages off the bed. He stood in the low ceilinged living room, the big gas stove providing warmth to its every corner. The mantel above the fireplace was covered with pictures of Minnie's two sons, one daughter, their children and grandchildren.

"Well, Minnie, are they all comin' here for Christmas this year?," John asked as he straighted the lace the pictures set on.

"I've not heard from a soul, so I just couldn't tell ye," she said, emerging from the back room with an armload of packages wrapped up in brown, slightly used grocery bags, their tell-tale creases showing. "I figgered I'd better mail everything. You know all my young'uns got families of their own now. They don't have time to come down here and see an old woman like me. Gilbert and Molly have finally got all their children out of the house and Frank and that wife of his just travel all the time. Now, my Sarah Jane, she's the smart one. She's goin' back to school."

"Have you ever thought about goin' to see any of them for Christmas? I know they've tried to get you to come."

"Honey, I've spent the last forty-eight Christmases here in this old house and I'm not goin to go gallivantin' around the countryside now."

She cast a glance at the picture of her dead husband, Joe. They would have been married forty-eight years come April and John figured that would have made her about seventy-one, from all that she had told him from time to time.

"Minnie, I'd better get goin'. School, you know. And I'll bet that family of yours will come draggin' in here any day and you'll be lucky to get 'em to leave." John L. loaded up the packages and headed toward school. It was only two days until Christmas vacation and eight days until Christmas. The tree that his fourth graders had decorated the week before was beginning to lose its needles and he would take it down after the kids left on Friday.

The school week finally ended with each room having little parties on Friday afternoon and John L. thought about the upcoming family gatherings and all the good food that the Christmas holidays afforded. Next year, he thought, he would talk Janie and the kids into going together to spend their Christmas money on some worthwhile cause and really try to help the kids understand the meaning of Christmas. John L. III, called "Lafe" (short for Lafayette) was eleven and old enough to understand that there were folks around him who had a lot less than he did. Louella was only eight and he knew that he would have to explain things to her.

As he drove up Lishes Branch that Friday afternoon, Aunt Minnie was out in the yard bustin' wood with an ax. Her light blue scarf wrapped tightly over her head covering all her hair except the bun in the back held in place by plastic combs, and her black and white wool coat buttoned to the bottom, she was oblivious to the cold wind that whipped down the holler.

"Minnie, let me help you with that wood. You know it's too cold to be out here doin' that," John L. said, as he walked over to where Minnie was leaning on the long ax handle, a sizeable pile of split black oak on each side of her.

"Oh, John, mind yer own business. A body's got to work a little or old Arther would get me and I'd cripple up for sure." Minnie laughed, straightened her back and winced only a little. "Besides, you just wait 'til some cold, dark night and your 'lectric goes off and you'll think of Minnie a settin' down here by a nice warm far."

"You're not the only one with wood cut, you know."

"I saw your woodpile a settin' out in the rain because that wife of yorn won't let you put it on the porch in the dry."

"She's sure got Janie figgered out," John thought to himself. "Minnie, how 'bout I cut your wood for you for the rest of the winter and you sell me that big iron kettle?" seeing the old salt vessel turned upside down by the edge of the porch.

"And what would I make my soap in?" she teased, taking her scarf off as she stepped onto the porch. "You know that belonged to my Granny Isaacs and I wouldn't part with it for nothin."

John L.'s hope of getting the kettle for Janie for Christmas disappeared. She had seen it many a time as they passed Minnie's house and wanted it for next summer's petunias.

"Have you heard from any of your kids?" John L. asked Minnie as he leaned against one of the square white porch posts. "Surely they've told you that they'll be down for Christmas."

"No, I've not heard a word and I doubt that I will. They got enough of this holler a growin' up in it and have gone on to bigger and better things."

Minnie was secretly proud of even the smallest successes of her children and would give them anything she owned, well, except her farm and house, and that was Minnie's forever. They had wanted her to sell it and move in with them, especially Sarah Jane. Each time one of the kids had mentioned moving, her "no" was more emphatic.

"Now, don't you worry. You'll hear from some of 'em any day." But Minnie was looking him squarely in the eye and she was not convinced by his words.

The remaining days until Christmas went quickly and John L. had a dozen things to catch up on, mainly a hunting trip or two out in S-tree country. Besides, Janie's parents had come down from Ohio for the week, and life with them was a little too much. But, Lafe and Louella saw their mom's parents very little and he guessed it was good for them to get reacquainted with their grandparents.

Squirrel season came to an unofficial end on the twenty-third as a hazy, morning sun gave way to a cold, gray afternoon with ever increasing drizzle as fog settled in on Lishes Branch and darkness came. Christmas Eve day brought more rain and a damp, cold wind that hinted of snow. That afternoon, John L. asked Janie if he couldn't take the kids over to his mom's for supper. That suited Janie fine, because she and her mom had come to an impasse as far as what to have for the Christmas dinner and neither was in a mood to cook.

Lafe and Louella visited Mommy and Poppy often and knew that a good meal was in store. They passed Aunt Minnie's on the way down Lishes Branch and a yellow light shown from a window in back of the house. Minnie had her quilting frame set up in the back room by the grate and always began her quilting with the first frost of fall. John L. only glanced at her house for a second and then wished that he hadn't, for he immediately felt sorry for Minnie. She was spending Christmas Eve alone.

John L.'s thoughts were interrupted as he turned up Little Wild Dog, the holler where he was raised and where his parents still lived. He pulled into the driveway and parked his truck behind his dad's. Lafe and Louella got out of the truck and flew to the front door hoping to surprise their grandparents and find a few unwrapped presents still lying around.

Aunt Minnie was still on John L.'s mind as his family sat down to supper. Only his mother noticed his distant behavior, but she didn't say a word about it, nor was she surprised when he disappeared out the back door, a tray covered with a blue-striped dish towel in hand. The rain had turned to big flakes of snow and the bridge over Little Wild Dog was just beginning to turn white on the edges. It was three and a half miles back to Minnie's and John L. didn't meet a single car. Yes, everybody was at home, each celebrating Christmas in their own way.

John L. knocked on the door at Minnies and stomped the snow off his boots.

"Now, you shouldn't have gone to all the trouble to bring food over here," Minnie fussed as she ushered him into the house and lifted the corner of the dish towel. "And that's your mommy's cookin', too," she said, as the unmistakable aroma of fried pork chops, apples and shuck beans filled the little living room. She went on and on about how much trouble John L. had gone to as he carried the tray back to the kitchen. "You know that they wouldn't have near as many at the potlucks at the Reformed Church if your mommy didn't go."

"Have you had dinner yet?" he plied, hoping she hadn't.

"No. I was fixin' to stir up some little somethin'." As Minnie was talking, John L. heard a car door slam in the driveway.

"Sit still, Minnie. I'll see who it is."

John L. peered through the glass in the front door, as Minnie, who had followed him into the living room, looked out the front window. A gray and blue striped van was parked in the yard and several people were walking toward the porch.

"Well, 'pon my honor," Minnie gasped with amazement, "it's my younguns and out on a night like this."

Sarah Jane was the first in the front door to give her mom a hug. She was followed by Gilbert and Molly. Frank brought up the rear with his wife, Margie.

After everybody was settled in the living room, the greetings and hugs exchanged, all was quiet for a few seconds except for the popping of the big gas heater and the nervous ticking of the mantel clock.

Gilbert began to explain that they had all wanted to surprise their mom at Christmas and just all got in Frank's new van and came down.

After inquiring about all the grandchildren and repeatedly giving thanks for the safe arrival of her family and on such slick roads, Minnie sank back into the faded pillows of her old rocking chair. "Won't we have a wonderful week here together! At least we will once Sarah Jane and I get to the store so we can get some cooking done. It'll be just like old times."

Gilbert and Frank looked out of the corner of their eyes at each other and Molly spoke up. "Oh, you won't need to do that. We're only staying tonight. You see one of Frank's old army buddies is letting us have his condo down in South Carolina for a week. We just couldn't pass it up. It's right on the beach."

Minnie stopped her slow rocking and her face froze as Sarah Jane slowly looked up at her and said, "You know we wouldn't want to cause you all that work and trouble. It would ruin your Christmas. Why, where would you put the six of us in this house?" Minnie's mind drifted back to a Christmas long ago when she and Joe and all three children had slept by the fire in this very room. On zero nights, she remembered stoking the fire every hour just to keep her family from freezing to death.

John L. got up and muttered something about it being nice to see everybody, wished Minnie a Merry Christmas, went out the door and headed for the truck. He hadn't looked her in the eye. He just couldn't.

The ground was white now and he zipped his coat up to his chin. It had gotten colder and the snow was falling hard, but in smaller flakes. It created its own silence and all was quiet but for the squeak of his boots on the white ground.

"Why did they even come?", he thought. "And why did they have to ruin it by telling her right off that they weren't staying? They could have gotten here earlier and they could have planned to stay a day or two." He felt badly for Minnie and never wanted to see any of her family again. He ducked his head against the wind and snow and walked to his truck. As he opened the truck door, he heard the screen door to Minnie's house shut and saw her motioning to him.

"Back that truck over here," ordered Minnie. "I've got something for you."

He got into the truck and backed it over to the porch taking care not to tear up the yard for only the top of the ground was frozen.

Minnie walked over to the edge of the porch, her arms crossed to keep her blue sweater wrapped tightly around her. John L. got out of the truck, its idle muffled by the deepening snow. Minnie nodded toward the iron kettle. "It's yours," she said, with an affirmation that would bear no argument.

John L. looked at her, studying her features, and without a word lifted the heavy kettle and rolled it onto the gray, wooden porch floor. Black dirt topped with snow was frozen to the rim where the kettle had rested on the ground.

He kissed Minnie's cheek and again she thanked him for the food as she turned and went into the house. He stood silently on the porch for a minute and then backed the truck, tailgate down, as close to the porch as he could get it and rolled the kettle into the truck bed. The place where the kettle had set on the ground already had a fine dusting of snow and within an hour would be like the rest of this world on Lishes Branch. He drove slowly out of Minnie's yard and on down the holler. The kettle jolted as he hit a hole or two, invisible under the thin layer of ice topped snow. No, Janie wouldn't use this kettle for flowers. Maybe he would let Minnie show the kids how soap was made or show them how to cook something in it this spring if he scrubbed and sanded it real good. He clenched the wheel a little tighter, angry at how time went by before you could get the things done that were important in life. It was too late for Minnie's kids and maybe for Janie, but he knew what he had to do. He was going to do it just for Minnie and for himself and the kids. Living in the mountains wasn't enough. He was going to teach Lafe and Louella and his kids at school how important it was to be of the mountains.

The twin beams of light from the truck shown through the falling snow and John L. sang a Christmas carol to himself as he turned up Little Wild Dog. The kettle shifted a little. No other gift would ever compare to the one that rode in the pickup bed. A gift as simple and unpretentious as its giver, but with sentiment as strong as the hands that had used it for these hundred years. A gift with a legacy as binding as the ties that held people like John L. and Minnie to this valley and these hills.

In twelve days, there would be another Christmas celebration on Lishes Branch. Yes, Old Christmas would be special this year. John L. would see to it.

THE IRON KETTLE

1. Aside from the reasons mentioned in the story, why do you think Aunt Minnie refused to leave her farm?

2. Why do you think Aunt Minnie's children left their home and went to the city? Have members of your family done this? Why?

3. Why do you think John L. stayed in his native community?

4. How do you think that John L. and Janie's views on life differ?

5. How do you think that Aunt Minnies quilting and methods of heating her home reflect her attitude toward the environment?

6. What does John L. mean by "being of the mountains?"

7. How are the holiday traditions of your family similar or different than those of Minnie or John L.?

8. What human qualities does the iron kettle represent?

RESEARCH: How did the tradition of Old Christmas evolve and where is it celebrated and why? What are the traditions of Old Christmas?

THE SLICKY ROCK

John L. stood in front of the grade school and watched the last of the buses disappear for the afternoon. The parking lot was still full of cars, though, and he knew why. Inservice. Some of them were O.K. but at the end of a long day, it was not John's idea of fun.

A voice from behind John startled him. "Are you staying?" asked Martin Blair, a fellow teacher who taught across the hall from John.

"I don't know. I only need one more inservice this year and there's several other times we can get one of them in. It's been a long day and the kids were wild. I don't blame them. It looks like spring is here.

"I can't stay. Daddy's brother is here from Oregon and he and Granny have a trip cooked up that they want me to take them on this afternoon. To tell you the truth, I dread it, but I promised them I would and Granny has looked forward to it all week."

"Where are you heading?"

"Down Station Camp. That's where Granny grew up and lived when she was first married. She wants to take Uncle Bill down there. She hasn't been in a good while. We've tried to get her to go several times but Bill is her favorite in the family and whatever he wants to do is alright with her. How about going with us? You know your way around down there and I'd never hear the end of it if we got lost or stuck or something and with all this rain we've had...."

"Enough said. After all, isn't that what makes for good teaching? You know, getting out and exploring and experiencing the environment," said John L. with a grin. "Just mention the woods on a day like this and I'm gone. Lead the way. Only thing, I've got to stop down the road here and get some gas."

A few minutes later, John L. pulled into Cal Adams's filling station with Martin right behind him. "Fill 'er up, Cal," John said as Cal himself came out of the station wiping his hand on a greasy rag.

"I thought you boys had a meetin' this afternoon," he said as he unscrewed the gas cap.

"What made you think that?" asked Martin as he cast a glance at John.

"Your wives were in here this morning on their way to Lexington and seems they mentioned somethin' about it," said Cal.

"Well, we're headin' down Station Camp with Granny Blair and Martin's Uncle Bill."

"Yeah, he was in here earlier with that new four wheel drive Suburban braggin' on what a truck it was and how it would outpull about anything in the mud. I washed it for him. Must be nice to have a ride like that," mused Cal.

A few minutes later, Martin and John pulled into Granny Blair's yard on Moores Creek. Bills shiny red Chevy was parked sideways across the yard so that no one who passed by would miss it. He and Granny were sitting on the from porch talking about old times.

"This is John L.," said Martin in the way of introduction to Bill. "He's going to go with us."

"And I'll say he brought just the vehicle to go in," said Bill as he walked over to John's Jeep. "Of course, it's not a new one, but it'll do fine."

"I thought for sure you'd want to take your Suburban, Uncle Bill," said Martin with more than a hint of sarcasm.

"You know, I really would, but the four wheel drive has been giving me some trouble and I'd hate to get us stranded down there. And if John doesn't mind.."

"No, I'd be honored to show you what a Jeep can do," John said flatly.

By that time, Martin had gone into the house in the pretense of getting a drink of water, but John knew that he was about ready to tell Bill all about what he could do with his shiny truck and probably would have if Granny Blair hadn't been there.

"Are we going to sit here and talk all day or what?" asked Granny. At that point she started down the steps and headed toward the Jeep. "Shore is a purty vehicle, John," she said, not having missed Bill's remark. Granny was eighty-eight but didn't miss much.

John had known Granny Blair all of his life and didn't remember her looking any different than she did today. She had on a flowered dress and black shoes. She was just barely five feel tall, but could make quick work of any job that a man twice her size would shun. Her fine features and dainty hands belied all the long hot days she had spent in the field and the miles of fence she had stretch around her place on Moores Creek. Since the death of her husband, some fifteen years before, Martin's dad and mom had helped on the farm, but until the past year or two, Granny had slowed up very little; none to hear her tell it. John had a great respect for Granny and admired her innate wisdom and insight into people. There was something about her that bothered him though. Something he and Martin had talked about from time to time. Granny and Martin didn't seem to be close at all, even though they lived just a field apart and saw each other almost every day. It seemed to be Martin's education that got in the way. He had been Granny's chosen one to take over the farm, but Martin hadn't shown much interest in it and although Granny never said so, John knew that she felt both disappointment and resentment over it. It was too bad because Martin and Granny were so much alike. The hamsters, fish and snakes in Martin's room at school were his animals just like Granny's chickens and cows were hers. They both were keen observers of the world, but just failed to connect on a day to day basis, John had figured. And that was too bad, he thought, because there was so much they could teach each other.

"Tell the boys about some of the fine work you're doin' out west," said Granny as the four headed through McKee and toward Kerby Knob. Not giving him a chance to answer, Granny proceeded, "if Bill hadn't a been out there when they had those fires last fall in Oregon, they'd still be burning, I'll tell you. He's about the best worker the government has." Granny's one weakness in the world was Bill. She believed all of his brags and tall tales and Martin and John noticed that he didn't do any anything to correct her. Martin had always figured it was because Bill was her first son and he had nearly died of the typhoid when he was two years old, but everybody was entitled to their favorites, he guessed.

As the Jeep turned off the blacktop and headed down Station Camp, Granny began to peer anxiously over the dashboard. John looked in her direction. "Not afraid we'll get stuck, are you, Granny?" he asked as they sloshed through one mudhole after another and the suspension bottomed out as they descended over rock ledges. He had never seen Granny this excited about anything as she related memories in rapid succession.

"I don't reckon. We're goin' downhill, ain't we? Besides, I've walked out of here many a time a carryin' one young'un and leadin' two more. I'm lookin' for where Uncle Cy's place was. I hear the heirs sold it and the new owners tore it down. My daddy helped build it. We've got to cross the creek first, though. Then we're there."

John shifted the Jeep into four wheel low as they forded the creek. Water lapped at the doors as Bill shifted nervously in the back seat.

"Right over there is where the Cy place set. Right there by that old apple tree. It's an Old Cannon tree. That's the best kind to make cider from. Let's stop here, John, if ye would. I'm thirsty."

"Mom, surely you're not goin' to drink out of that creek," said Bill.

"No, you fool. There's a dandy spring up behind the house or at least there used to be. It was the best one around and the water was real cold, like right out of a cave or something." Granny strode off through the Indian grass, blackberry briars and beggar lice to get a drink with the others following as close behind as they could.

"This is National Forest land now," said Bill proudly as they climbed a little ways up the hill to where Granny thought the spring to be. He had studied the topo maps continually since they had left Granny's house that afternoon and by now professed to be an expert on most of the Kentucky River drainage.

"Well, if it's government land, then why ain't they kept this spring cleaned out, is what I'd like to know?" asked Granny as she cleaned leaves out of the spring and waited for the water to clear. After a while she dipped her hands in the water and took a drink. "Just like it used to be. Cold and sweet as ever. They never was any farming or mining above this spring as I remember. The timber was cut, but that was all. When I lived on the creek, this whole bottom was planted in corn."

"The government protects it now," Bill chimed in.

"They need to do better. That Old Cannon tree has gone to ruin. You don't find a good Old Cannon just everyday. I'm goin' to get a little sprig off of it and see if I can graft it," said Granny as she got out a worn

Case knife and cut a switch off the tree. As they once again got into the Jeep and drove slowly along the rutted road, Granny told them about Uncle Cy.

"His inheritance from Grandpaw was a millstone. Grandpaw took great pride in that stone. His daddy had brought it from Russell County, Virginia, years before. A good millstone was a great thing to have. Better'n any kind of education because if you had a good mill and was honest, you could always make a decent living. Uncle Cy had a little mill right down here on the creek and he and Aunt Lucy ran it for years. He ground corn and wheat and they wasn't a bit of grit in it and just as fine as powder if that was the way you wanted it. One spring night it stormed and rained awful to this world. It came a big tide and washed that mill plum away, millstone and all. Uncle Cy was just sick over it and couldn't sleep a wink. Finally the whole family got together and we started down the creek a huntin' for that stone. It was on a wooden shaft and that had helped float it. We hunted all day and found it in a shoal almost buried in the mud. I bet it had gone over a mile. Never did find any of the mill. It wasn't a month before Uncle Cy was back in business. I've never seen a body so happy to find anything.

The road began to leave the creek bottom and the Jeep slipped and slid as it climbed the hill that would take them over Chestnut Ridge and down to where the old Blair homeplace was. As they reached the top of the hill and drove along the firmly packed sand, Granny gasped, "Where have all the trees gone?"

"This is a timber sale area," said Bill. "The trees are harvested in areas like this. It's one of many ways the forest and its products are useful to society."

"Maybe so, but it's ugly. Reminds me of when they cut the timber when I was a girl. It was ugly then, too. You talk about the woods like they was a factory or something. With all the houses and parking lots these days, you'd think they'd leave a place where a body could just come and think and the animals could live. The woods was full of purty flowers when I came back here years ago - bluebells, flags, all kinds of things. A rabbit couldn't get through that bresh now."

"They'll let this area grow back and maybe cut it again someday. The forest is more productive when light can get to it," said Bill, looking up from his topo map.

Granny turned her mouth down at the corners. "Ginseng and flags don't grow good in the light."

"I'll bet things haven't changed a bit down at the old homeplace," said Martin trying to change the subject.

"I don't know," said Bill. "Things don't stay the same forever."

John looked in the rear view mirror at Martin. He was giving Bill an icy stare and mouthing silently the words, "shut up." Bill ignored him totally.

"Who owns the old place now, Mom?" asked Bill.

"Your cousin, Sue Ann. I don't know what use she'll ever make of it. That husband of hers will never leave Dayton." She paused for a minute. "Bill , let's you and me see if we can't buy the homeplace, that is if they haven't let it fall down by now."

"Now, Mom, what would you want with that place way down in here in the middle of nowhere?"

"I might want to live in it."

"And who would take care of you and do stuff for you?'

"Me, that's who," she said. "The same one that always has."

Martin glared at Bill again and then looked out the window as he wondered what life would have been like down here half a century ago. He had a special kinship with this place and often had dreamed about coming here to get away from things. Funny how people don't appreciate the things that are within their grasp, he thought, as he contemplated what Bill had just said. Bill didn't appreciate his roots. He never had. That's probably why he moved away to start with or more likely the reason he had never and would never come back.

John L. looked over at Granny. He knew that she would be crushed if the old homeplace was gone. He wanted to turn around, but that wasn't an option. As they rounded the bend, there it was, a little worse for the wear and almost lost in the long, late afternoon shadows. It was the house that Granny's children had been born in; the place she still regarded as home. Granny didn't say a word, but her hand tightened around the door handle as if she could not wait for the Jeep to stop so she could set foot once again on the land that she had once called her own. John stopped the Jeep in the middle of the road in front of the house and everyone got out and looked at the landmark of a former time that stood before them. It was surrounded by briars and sumac bushes still retaining their seedpods from the previous fall.

"Well, what are we standing here for?" asked Bill. "Let's all go in. "I mean, that's what we came for, isn't it?"

Granny stood her ground. "You all go. I'm stayin' here."

Bill was clearly annoyed at this point. "What? After we've brought you all the way down here?"

"That's right," said Granny. "I'm going to remember the place just like it was when we lived there. I'll only guess what the inside looks like now." At that, Bill strode off through the yard, camera in hand, and made his way toward the front porch.

Granny watched him and then turned to John L. and Martin who were leaning against the Jeep. "Boys," she said, "there's one other place that I'd like to go while he's messing around in there."

"Just tell us where," said Martin.

Granny continued. "When I was a girl, there was a place just a little ways down the creek where me and all the other kids would go on hot summer days. It's call the slicky rock. The creek bottom there is solid rock and real slick. We'd take a run and then slide on it. Mommy didn't worry about us too much 'cause the water wasn't over a couple inches deep. It was a natural crossing in the creek. You could take a wagon and team across it any time of the year even in the spring when the other fords was too deep."

"Do we need to drive there?" asked John.

"No, it's just around this bend. Let's walk."

"Looks like somebody's been through here with some kind of machinery," said John L. as they walked in the recently made tracks.

As they rounded the bend, Granny said, "right up there is the crossing." As they neared the creek, she stopped in her tracks. Everybody looked down into the creek. What had been a smooth expanse of black rock was now chipped, broken and crushed into jagged pieces. Two pieces of metal pipe had been laid on the creek bottom and tons of white limestone covered the pipes in the name of a new road. Across the creek was the culprit; a giant yellow dozer, its mandibles raised and motionless in the air like a frozen insect waiting for man to awaken it so it could pursue its diet of ancient rock and young saplings. The rhododendron and laurel bushes that had lined the creek for centuries were scraped and mangled. Even though their leaves were still green, this would be the last spring that they would grace the cool banks of Station Camp. The water echoed with an unnatural roar as it traveled through the twelve foot length of pipe.

After staring silently at the scene for a couple of minutes, Granny said in a quiet voice, "they used to be all kinds of round creek rocks up the way a little. I don't know why they had to bring these white ones in." She obviously had seen enough and the trio turned and walked back up the road toward the old Blair house.

For the first time, John saw Granny as an old woman. Her steps were not as sure as they had been when she cut the switch off the apple tree. He thought that it was ironic that the slicky rock had been there for eons and then had been destroyed in the relative speck of a lifetime of probably the only person who cherished this place and its memories. She stopped and dipped her handkerchief in a small clear stream that trickled across the road on which they walked. Later she would wrap it around the apple branch to keep it alive until she returned home to Moore's Creek and the safe haven of her farm. A scarlet tanager cocked its head as it sat perched in a box elder tree. Maybe it, also, was not attuned to the new echo of roaring water and diesel engines.

Just as they reached the Jeep, Bill emerged from the house and said, "I understand that they're making a new road down the creek from here to get access to a new development over across the ridge. Let's go have a look."

Granny, Martin and John just looked at one another and got in the Jeep while Bill waited for them to answer. Finally, John started the motor and rolled down the window and said to Bill, "watch while I turn around here and don't let me get in that big mudhole." John turned the wheel this way and that as he turned the vehicle around. He looked behind him and Bill was still there motioning him on back. John grinned to himself and just couldn't resist gunning the Jeep just a little. Mud went flying in Bill's direction. Everyone tried their best not to laugh when he opened the door and got in. He mumbled all the way home about dirt on his camera lens and fools that couldn't drive in the mud.

When they arrived at the farm on Moores Creek, Bill headed straight to his room to change clothes. Granny laughed. "That mud was the best thing that's happened to him in a while."

"Well Granny," said Martin, "if we're ever going to have any cider we better get that tree planted."

Granny hesitated a minute as if lost in thought and then headed across the yard with her grandson as John watched from the porch. Martin stopped as they opened the gate to the field and handed Granny something. It was a piece of the slicky rock. Martin didn't know John had seen him pick it up when they were at the creek. Granny turned it over and over in her hand. The rock wasn't slick anymore and it just looked like any old rock except to her and Martin. She put her arm around his shoulder and John heard her say just as they went out of earshot, ""Martin, let's you and me see if we can't buy up some of the old place and fix it up a little."

John didn't hear his reply, but saw him nod his head, yes.

THE SLICKY ROCK

1. Why do you think Granny Blair wants to buy the old homeplace? Do you think that she and Martin will actually do so?

2. In most all areas of the country, there are debates about how public land should be used. How should these questions be decided? Should local residents have a say? How can the environment and business interests be balanced?

3. Flags is a term that is used in Appalachia for members of the Iris family. What local names are given to plants or animals in your area that aren't necessarily the "official names?"

RESEARCH: Old Cannon is a variety of apple used to make apple cider. It is considered to be a "heritage" plant, one that is passed from generation to generation and not readily available at a store or nursery. Interview folks in your area that have gardened for years and see if they have varieties of plants or vegetables that have been in their family for generations. What are some of these varieties? Why might it be valuable to save those species or varieties?

TROUBLE ON DATHA CREEK

John L. and Ike leaned against the rough rocky face of a damp, limestone cliff and looked down the steep hill where one hundred feet below, narrow Datha Creek rushed over round stones to be lost in the cold, blue-gray waters of Catkin. The narrow ledge on which they walked had no doubt been a trail for as long as man or animal had roamed the rhododendron covered slopes of this holler that eventually widened and ended where Catkin poured into War Fork at the Bob Lakes place. It would be joined by countless other nameless tributaries, some as clear as glass and inhabited by blind fish; others sluggish and sterile with red acid and silt from "reclaimed" mines before joining the muddy Kentucky at Beattyville.

The day was warm and humid for April and the bluebirds darted from hill to hill in search of a home in a few old locust posts, that except for some moss covered rocks, were the only visible remains of an old homestead tucked in a cove at the confluence of the two streams. The columbine blossoms dangled with perfect elegance from slender stems rooted in the smallest cracks in the inch wide shelves in the limestone. The more unlikely the home, the more beautiful the blossom in its attempt to mate and survive. Here and there, under the shade of wet cliffs that dripped, except in January and dog days, were patches of pure white trilliums with leaves and blossoms of three.

"I've often imagined that I might inspire my students to get out in a place like this but I never really thought they would inspire me to do it," said John L. "Guess that's where I have a lot to learn."

"Yep, you do. "Some of the kids I've got in class this year inspire me to leave school before I get there of the mornin'," mused Ike, never cracking a smile and all the time scanning the cliffline on the other side of the holler. "Read that paper you've got there again."

"Do you really believe this story for the truth?" John L. asked as he got the folded piece of white paper from his pocket.

"Maybe. I've had a lot of boys from down in here in class and they're always full of wild tales, but there's truth to a lot of the things they say. Makes life more interesting if you believe."

John had asked his fourth graders to bring in a family story as part of a writing project and the results had been interesting. Some had brought legends from Civil War times and another had told about daddy's experience in Nam. One little girl told about her aunt's new boyfriend that she wasn't supposed to know about. However, the story John held in his hand was unusual and had come from an equally unusual source. Billy Myers had brought it. The quiet kid on the front row who gaped and squinted at whatever John wrote on the board. The kid who had never shown a bit of imagination and had never clamored for attention.

When Billy had read his story in class, some listened in wonderment. Others accused him of making it up. Billy declared it was true. It involved a treasure of gold that was hidden in a cave in this valley. Billy's grandfather had received a letter from a man that he had not seen in over fifty years but they had been childhood friends here on Datha. The odd thing about the letter was that it had not been mailed by the old man, but by his son. It seems that the son had found the letter in his father's things after he had passed away. Even though the letter had been written some years before, he mailed it to Billy's grandfather anyway.

John held the paper in the afternoon sun and began to read the letter that was in Billy's story.

> I'll bet you'd never thought you'd hear from me after all these years. I was thinking the other day about our growing up years down in the Datha Holler and something came across my mind that I never have told anybody about. You know I always did like to explore around in the hills. Well, it was in the summertime and I had walked a way up on the hill. It was real hot and daddy and my brothers were getting the garden laid by. I couldn't have been over five or six year old.

Anyway, I sat down up there to rest and there was a place in the hill with cool air blowing out of it. I moved a few rocks and squeezed back in there. It was a pretty good sized cave. I was scared of caves for mommy had always told me there was snakes in caves, so I didn't stay in it long. When I got home, I told Grandpaw about it. Mommy would have whipped me if I'd have told her. Grandpaw thought a while and told me he had heard of such a cave on the hill up there, but had never seen it hisself. He said that his daddy told him that years ago the Dathas had lived in that same holler and the story was that they had hid a fortune in gold somewhere around.

Grandpaw said they were from New Orleans and had been involved in politics way back when the French owned the territory west of here. They had helped out some folks from Kentucky that had come to New Orleans by way of the river. They eventually got a hold of a lot of land here in the county-several thousand acres.

Me and Grandpaw went back up to that cave not long before he died. It was hard to find and it was easy to get lost in because of the way the passages branched off and curved around. There was a room with a waterfall in it and somebody had carved out the tunnels with a pick and there were numbers scratched on the walls. We explored around a little and when we left we covered the entrance back up. I always meant to go back there, but I know I never will now. I always knew you were kin to the Dathas some way or another, so I thought I would tell you about it. Maybe I'll get over to see you one of these days. I don't drive anymore, because I can't see too good, but some of the children might bring me.

Your old friend,
Elton

"I'd say there's mighty little chance of us finding that cave," said Ike. "If there is such a cave we'd have heard something about it. The entrance could have got covered up when they logged this place years ago, too."

"Well, we'll not find it standing here talking about it. That's for sure."

As the afternoon went on, John and Ike hunted the hillside high and low, crawling over every cliff and becoming exited every time they found what would turn out to be a rock house that dead ended in a wall of rock.

"Now let's use our heads," said Ike. "If you were six years old and you came up here from that garden spot in the holler and wanted to find a cool place on a hot day, where would you go?"

"I'd get out of the sun. I guess that would be on the north side of the hill."

"Right. And if your mommy didn't want you exploring around, you'd get out of sight of the house, too."

"I guess that means we've been looking in too obvious a place," said John as they headed around the mountain out of sight of the waters of Datha Creek.

The north side of the hill seemed to take nature back a month or so. There were no patches of sun and the columbines, trailing arbutus and trilliums found this habitat too cold and damp for their liking. The oak leaves that had shaded this hillside on hot July afternoons now only made the trail slippery and John and Ike had to use one hand for support against the hillside as they continued their search.

As John looked up this holler, he saw that it ended in a narrow cove with a small waterfall that was undoubtedly fed by some wet weather spring somewhere on the hillside. He sat down, his legs tired from hiking around the mountain all day. "It'd be a lot easier if one leg was shorter than the other to do this type of walking," he said to Ike. "I'm wore out."

"Me, too," said Ike as he leaned against a buckeye tree." I'm about ready to chalk this one up to legend and just say I've enjoyed the scenery. "Those Myerses are windy anyway. Billy's uncle T.R. could blow up an onion sack."

The sun was low enough in the sky now that only the ridgetops were enjoying warmth and the cold dampness of the forest seem to rise from the black earth and give the evening back to a winter that was seemingly gone earlier in the day. As John stood up to start the long hike back to the truck, he noticed that across the holler from him was a small stream trickling out of the hillside. "Let's go over and check out that little cliff, Ike."

"Might as well. We've checked out the rest of them. What's one more?"

It was only about a three minute trek as the two clambered down one hillside and up the next. As Ike lead the way up the hill, he turned around and said, "feel that cold air coming down from that cliff. I bet we've hit pay dirt, this time."

The cliff looked like a blank wall from even a short distance away, but there was indeed a draft of cool, dry air coming from somewhere. But try as they might, a cave entrance did not present itself.

"Ike, give me a boost." I think that air is coming from above our heads." John placed one boot in Ike's cupped hands and was lifted about three feet higher. "I see where the air is coming from, but it's just a narrow horizontal crack in the rock not big enough for a dog to get through." Ike lowered him back down.

"There's a cave here somewhere if we can just figure out how to get into it," said Ike.

With renewed enthusiasm, the two searched every inch of the cliffline. Just as they were about to give up, Ike yelled, "come over here and help me move this rock. I think I've found something."

John helped Ike give the rock a shove. It moved surprisingly easy. Beyond them was a gaping black hole. Ike reached for his flashlight and he and John wasted no time entering what was a fair sized room of a cavern with about an eight foot ceiling. The dirt on the floor was well packed but there was no sign that anyone had been there recently or for years for that matter.

"Do you think we've found it? I mean the one in the letter," John asked excitedly as he followed Ike and the beam of yellow light deeper into the cave.

"Let's see if we can find the room with the waterfall that the letter talked about."

They wove their way around rocks that jutted out from the wall and ducked at points where the ceiling was lower, but the path back into the heart of the mountain seemed well defined.

John noticed an old brown Coke bottle lying on the floor. "Well, someone's been here, but it was a long time ago. We'll pick that up on the way out. Your light is getting dim and it's the only one we have. I think we'd better come back tomorrow with your miner's light and some candles and rope." John did not like caves and the thought that one could get lost had crossed his mind.

As they backtracked, John was reassured when he saw the old Coke bottle and he started to pick it up but decided against it since it would just be one more thing to carry. Besides, he could get it tomorrow. Right now, he was just excited that he and Ike had maybe found the long lost Datha cave. His concentration was broken by something that first he considered unusual and then sent chills along his spine. "Ike, didn't we already pass that brown Coke bottle once?"

"Yep. Maybe they had a party and there's two of them."

John accepted this explanation for the moment, but his hands were starting to sweat. It wasn't a minute more before his worst fears were realized. The Coke bottle, again. He looked at Ike with apprehension, for he too, had realized that there was only one bottle and they were looking at it for the third time in two minutes.

"Now, just wait a minute before you come to any conclusions," Ike said as he looked at John. "We've not gone over a hundred feet into this cave and we're not lost. No way. Just follow me."

Ike started off on what looked like the path they had taken on their way in but it was only a minute before the bottle showed up again. He looked at John and raised his eyebrows.

John slumped back against the wall, all the while noticing that the yellow beam from the flashlight was growing dimmer by the minute. He looked about frantically and said, "let's go this way." He started down what he hoped was the passage to freedom. Only twenty feet down the corridor, the floor sloped upward and met the ceiling and he knew this wasn't the way. He turned and ran back to where he had started, scraping his back against the low ceiling. Bats started to fly, awakened from a winter sleep. He covered his head with his hands and fell to the floor.

"Now, settle down," said Ike. "We're not beat yet."

John, all the while was looking for another passage to try. He started off in the opposite direction, his hands on the walls on either side of him pushing himself as fast as he could go. Just fifteen feet this time. Another dead end. He started to turn around and then he called to Ike. "Come here. I think I see light."

Ike ventured down the narrow passage and sure enough, it was the fading light of day. "I'll bet that's the crack in the rock you saw when I boosted you up."

"But we can't get through it," said John. His thoughts were of spending the rest of his life yelling through a crack in a rock and he knew that no one would ever hear him. "No one knows where we are," he thought, "and we've crossed the creek so many times today, they'd never find us even if they found the truck. We'll starve to death." There was a slow steady drip of water somewhere out of the range of their light.

Ike shut his eyes. "We've been going around in circles, that's for sure. I just don't understand it." He walked back to the brown Coke bottle and looked all around him at the floor. "Here's our boot tracks over and over again." He scanned the floor again with the light then turned it off and sat down by John.

John felt the sheer horror as he knew when the light was gone, their chances were nil of getting out of this dark prison because each step they would take could lead to only farther back into the unknown. How long would the light last? How long would it be before their families realized something was wrong? He was unaware of any word in the English language that described his feelings right now. "After all the adventures we've had in our lives and reckless things we've done, did you think it would end like this?" asked John.

"We're not done for yet. Just let me think."

John had a lot of confidence in Ike to get them out of messes, but it was obvious that even Ike's seemingly infallible sense of direction and knowledge of the woods was of no use in this world of no sun, mountains or rivers. It was an unrelenting prison unwilling to give Ike and John the path to the top of the earth.

John thought of all the unfinished projects and future plans that he had taken for granted just a few minutes ago. He felt that they had disappeared into nothingness just as he and Ike had.

Ike turned on the light again, its feeble beam flickering, and shone it around their prison made of sharp rocks that knew nothing of wind, day or night. The transparent cave crickets scattered, their long feelers finding the way for them.

Man had not altered this environment. He had not moved rocks to make roads and fields. It was a terrain that defied ordinary logic. Ike continued to shine the light on each nook and cranny and abruptly it went out. He clicked the switch again and again but he knew the effort was futile.

John sat quietly by Ike and shut his eyes and then realized that it didn't matter if eyes were shut or open. It was just as dark one way as the other. "What now?" he asked.

"Don't know. Guess we'll just sit here awhile."

"Like we have a choice," thought John. In the distance, the slow drip of water was deafening to John's ears. Was it dripping on a rock or in a pool? He didn't know and didn't care, but he focused on the sound and noticed that the drip was getting faster. John thought that if he had a watch that glowed in the dark, he could time the drips. Then another thought. How many drips to ten heartbeats? At first; five. Then, ten and a few minutes later too many to count. John wondered why he was focusing on this small sound and came to the conclusion that he was in the first stages of losing his mind. And then from his clouded subconscious, the realization came that water was entering the cave. It must be raining. At first, it was comforting to have a connection with the outside world besides air. Then there was chilling thought that people had drowned in caves not far from here.

"Hear that water," he said matter of factly to Ike. "Now, we're gonna drown."

Ike didn't comment at first, undoubtedly lost in his own thoughts. Then he said, "I've never known water to flow back into a cave. It usually runs toward the entrance."

"Or sinks in a hole or fills up the cave before it runs out," said John. "I never did like caves anyway and I sure don't like caves with water in them." Time seemed to have no meaning in this place and after a few minutes or a few hours there was a steady pour of water that seemed to grow closer and louder all the while.

John didn't know if he had dozed off, but he was suddenly aware of Ike talking to him and instantly he knew why. As he straightened up against the cold rock, his hand touched even colder water. The water was here! The cave was filling up.

"Now maybe this a good thing," said Ike. "This water may run out of here and we can follow it" Somehow his voice did not convince John.

John and Ike both instinctively stood up as if to avoid the rising stream. But avoid it they could not as the frigid water rose around their ankles and then their knees. "At least you have an advantage here," said John. "You're taller." Then, in a more serious mode, he looked in Ike's direction and said, "I can't feel my feet anymore."

"Me neither."

For the next while the two talked about how there was no need for panic at this point, there was simply no choice but to stand and wait. But wait on what? Wait to drown? Wait on someone to come to find them?

The water was up to their waists now and it didn't seem to be flowing anywhere, just getting deeper. John noticed, though, that something had changed inside the cave. It seemed to be getting lighter or was he seeing things. "Look at the wall over there," he said to Ike. "Do you see light?

"Maybe."

They stared at the spot and a thin line of light was appearing on the cave wall. But from where? As they looked down the passage behind them, the answer was evident. It was light coming from the thin crack in the cave face that they had seen earlier. It was dawn. They turned and looked again at the inch high line of light on the cave wall. A name was etched in that small space. It was "A. Datha." And next to it was an arrow. Half walking, half swimming, they wasted no time in heading in the direction that the arrow pointed. After a hundred feet or so that had seemed like a mile, the water got shallower and the moist air of the outside world met them. The damp smell of the woods and the first light of morning filled their eyes and ears.

John and Ike both sat down on a rock at the mouth of Datha Cave. Neither said a word, but just sat and took in deep breaths of fresh air. The outside world was filled with wonderful smells and a cacophony of sounds that would guide their way back home.

As they drove back toward Sand Gap, Ike berated himself over and over again. "It'd take a fool to go in a cave and just look straight ahead, but that's what we did. If we'd have got lost in there, we'd have to wear bags over our heads for a long time, just to let people know how stupid we were."

John thought to himself that didn't sound like too bad of a punishment considering what could have happened. "You know what we did was came through a small passage and into a bigger one, and when we started back, we stayed in the big passage and it went in circles. Sorta like taking a ramp onto an interstate.

It's obvious where you're headed at that point. But, when we came back, we didn't realize we needed to take the ramp and stayed on the big road instead." Ike shook his head, but didn't comment on John's analogy.

The gold of the Datha's was far from their thoughts as they drove along U.S. 421. They each knew that someday they would go back, but not tomorrow or even next week. It just didn't seem important. It would wait. John rolled down the truck window and felt the cool wind on his face and occasionally heard the frogs holler as they crossed low country. He knew he was alive and was grateful to be that way. The future plans and unfinished projects were coming back into his mind now; a mind that had been washed clean by fear. He knew that no matter where he traveled that the experience of the Datha cave would be with him and Ike forever.

TROUBLE ON DATHA CREEK

1. Do you think that there is truth to the legends of lost fortunes hidden in caves or buried in the mountains of Appalachia? What is one of the most famous of these legends?

2. When and what part of the United States was once owned by the French?

3. Why is it a mistake to look just straight ahead when exploring a cave?

4. Can you deduce how the trillium got its name?

5. Have you ever seen a cave fish and why do you think they are blind?

6. What makes water from some mining operations red and what is meant by the water was sterile?

7. Under what weather conditions should you not enter a cave?

8. Are there times of the year when you should not enter a cave because the bats shouldn't be disturbed? What seasons are these?

REBECCA'S LAMENT

"You can't beat a day like this for wanderin' around in the woods," said Rob to his friend John L.

Since when is huntin' turkey the same as wanderin' around in the woods?

Rob grinned. "Turkey ain't a sport, it's a pastime. I've not even seen but one or two of them during turkey season, so I know my chances aren't too good for taking one home.

"I think the trees have leafed out a lot since yesterday, 'cause it's been so warm," said John L.

Rob looked over his shoulder as the two walked up Big Hill on the old wagon road on the east side of Cowbell Creek. "Yeah, it's been a little too warm and from the look of those clouds over there, we'll get some rain."

"Those clouds don't mean a thing. My Uncle Russ says the weather don't always go over Big Hill. Sometimes, it'll snake around to the south and go down Birch Lick to McKee or it'll go up Owsley Fork or Red Lick toward Drip Rock or Irvine."

They walked on for awhile and soon the early April warmth gave way to a nippy breeze and white clouds came tumbling over the mountain from the west. "Don't believe we'll make it to the truck," said Rob, glancing at the sky as they walked a little faster. The wind began to pick up and whistle through the tiny, new maple leaves. As it blew stronger, the small oaks moved awkwardly with each gust while their ancestors swayed from side to side. The far side of the holler became obscured from view as a curtain of rain disguised as a blanket of gray fog moved across the valley with an ever increasing roar. The rain fell first in big drops as Rob and John

L. bounded for the shelter of a nearby cliff. Just as they stepped onto the dry sandy floor of this rockhouse, it came in torrents. Within a few minutes, water dripped, then flowed in a steady stream over the top of the cliff creating puddles at their feet.

"Think it'll rain?" asked Rob as he cupped his hands under the small waterfall and splashed it on his face.

John L. sat down on a flat rock and gazed out at the rain, which was now falling straight down, having calmed the wind and cooled the air. "This is the best excuse I've had just to sit in a long time. There's something about it that leaves you free to let your mind wander." John marveled at the bright green of the newly leafed-out maples and poplars in contrast to the branches of the hickories and oaks still mimicking the leaden sky of a winter gone by. The white dogwood blossoms glistened in the rain, but something unusual had caught John L.'s eye.

"Hey Rob, look at that pink dogwood down there." John L. pointed to a tree a little ways down the hill. It was sure enough a dogwood with pink blossoms. It didn't have as many flowers as the white trees, but it looked to be a dogwood, nonetheless.

"Reckon he's a store bought feller?"

"No..., no, I don't think so. Not way up here. Seems like I've read that they do occur in the wild, but not very often. Anyway, I've seen a lot of dogwoods in these hills and it's the first one like it I've seen.

"Granny puts nails in the ground around her snowball bushes and it turns 'em colors. Reckon there's some kind of mineral in the ground or more likely an old wire fence? That's prob'ly what it is. You're the most curious one about plants that I ever did see."

John L. shot Rob a withering look and was not about to have his find accounted to a rusty piece of wire.

When the rush of the creek below could be heard as the rain slacked off, John stepped from under the cliff and climbed down the bank to get a closer look at the tree. He picked a flower from the tree and examined it.

"It's a pink one, alright. Maybe you'll be famous if we ever get out of this holler and back to the Gap," mocked Rob.

The rain finally stopped and a cool wind blew through the trees showering the two with water as they slipped and slid in the mud on their way back to the truck.

"I'll bet this road was better than this a hundred years ago," commented John as he sloshed through one puddle after another. "You know this used to be the main road through here before they built the blacktop road back in the 1920's. I've heard about when they first took cars over this road and the suspension would be plum wore out before they got to the bottom of the Big Hill. Daddy's told me that even when they built the new road they used to have to back the car up the steepest part because it wouldn't pull it goin' forward."

"I know they took cannons and wagons up this road during the Civil War and I can sure see why the Battle of Big Hill was fought in the fall during dry weather," said Rob. Wouldn't 'a been nobody up for it if the weather had been this wet. Did I ever tell you my great-great Granddaddy was killed at Vicksburg? Daddy took a vacation down there one time just because he'd heard his people talk about it so many times. He got a lot of mileage out of that trip. For years, he told everybody in the family about how he walked over the battlefield. You'd have thought he fought it hisself. He's about tellin' stories the way you are about plants. He knows a lot of 'em." Rob grinned at his analogy.

The red pickup appeared in the distance, looking all the better for its bath.

"Reckon we can get out of here in all this mud?" asked John L. as Rob got the truck turned around in the road with more spinning than steering.

"Not a doubt in my mind. Better lock in the hubs unless you want to walk some more."

The truck bounced and lurched from side to side as it crept up the sandstone ledges that alternated with miry level stretches. John studied the pink dogwood flower and wondered about its beginnings.

"Guess we've had the lick now," said Rob as he pushed in the clutch and the truck slid to a halt. A slide of shiny mud three feet deep was blocking the road. "But, then again, what do we have to lose?" He popped the clutch and the Chevy plowed ahead only to be stopped very short with its engine racing and wheels spinning. The slide was only seven or eight feet long but it might as well have been a hundred.

The two men climbed out of the cab and swung themselves into the bed of the truck and jumped out the back to avoid being mired up themselves. "Johnny Allen lives right over in the next holler," said Rob. "He's got a blade on his truck and he'll have us out of here in no time."

About an hour's walk later, a long, low white house came into view. It had a chimney in the middle and looked like it might have been a log house that had been weatherboarded and added to as the family grew. Chickens scattered across the yard as Rob and John climbed the bowed board steps and knocked on the screen door. Two small faces appeared around the corner and a flurry of legs disappeared through the room toward the back of the house.

"Mommy, there's some men out there," one of them hollered as they followed behind a skinny woman with a ponytail, wiping her hands on a dish towel as she came to the door.

"Hey, Rob," she greeted. "If you're lookin' for my old man, he ain't here. He took the truck and went huntin' early this morning. Don't know when he'll be back. Maybe in a little while; maybe next week."

"Well, if you don't care, we'll just set on the porch and wait a while on him. We've got the truck stuck and are goin' nowhere anyway."

"You'll come in and have some dinner is what you'll do. How'd it look for us to be eatin' and you all settin' out here. Granny, set two more places." Donna yelled into the house and then muttered, "the old woman's deaf when she wants to be. I'll prob'ly have to do it myself. Now come on in. I know your hungry if you walked into this holler."

As John and Rob sat down at the table, the two small white faces sized up the situation from the doorway. "Young'uns, set down," Donna yelled at them without even looking up and they scurried to the table.

"This is Granny," Donna said of an old woman sitting at the end of the table. "We live here in her house with her. Somebody has to look after her, you know."

The old woman nodded and smiled to John and Rob and studied them with dark eyes that were a stark contrast to her white hair and fair skin.

John L. guessed that she was in her eighties as he watched the strong hands pick up one dish after another and fill her plate. "I'm John," he said quietly, glancing in her direction.

"I'm Lellie. Glad you could have some dinner with us this evenin'." The kids giggled as they kicked each other under the table all the while escaping threatening glares from their mother. Afterward, everybody went out and sat on the front porch except for Lellie who appeared after doing the dishes. She sat on a pillow and rocked slowly in the swing and once again eyed Rob and John L.

"Now who are you boys again?" she asked.

"I'm Rob Lainhart and this is a friend of mine, John L.

"Where are ye from?"

"Sand Gap."

Lellie cocked her head to one side and seemed to ponder saying anything else. After a minute, she said, "I knew some Lainharts once."

"Yeah?" said Rob. "Who were they?"

"Don't remember the names. But, no matter. Was a long time ago, anyway."

It began to get dark in the holler and Rob moved out of his chair to the steps and whittled on a piece of cedar that Johnny had left on the edge of the porch for that very purpose. Lellie sat and sang to herself while she looked and stemmed a mess of greens from the field and creesies from the creek. John wished to himself that he had brought something to tape Lellie's song. It would be a good rainy afternoon rest time listening activity for the kids at school. He vowed he would come back and do it if he ever got out of this place and back home anytime soon.

"Don't know where that Johnny is," said Donna. "Prob'ly stuck in a creek some'ers. He's sorta like Rob here. He don't care for nothin' when he's behind the wheel of that truck.

"I sure did like that song," said John.

Lellie looked up and smiled. "I didn't know you was a list'nin."

"How 'bout singin' it for me again?"

"Go on. Sing it for him," said Donna. Be glad he likes to hear them old songs. I sure don't!"

"Well, alright. I may have forgot some of the words, though. Hit's been a long time since I've sung it before tonight." Lellie set her pan of greens aside and begin to sing as she rocked slowly in the swing.

I sing a song of sorrow.
A song of woe.
I sing this song my love to you,
For from here I go.

I here the guns a firin'.
The awful cannons roar.
The blue clad men are marchin'
And they stop at our door.

The spring it was a wet one,
And the summer so dry.
There is no food for us.
I fear we will die.

I'm goin' back to Owsley
My kin are there.
I'm leavin' you a present
For all I can't bear.

Remember the springtime
When we were so young.
And through the deep forest
All day we did run.

And on the high mountain
Where the red tree did bloom
I told you that I loved you
And I'd marry you soon.

I know you still love me
And that when you return
To that place you will go
And my secret you'll learn.

When Lellie was done, no one spoke a word. Even Donna's kids were entranced by the minor mode of the song they had just heard.

"That was beautiful, Lellie," said John L. "about the best I've ever heard. Where'd you learn that?"

"Oh, I don't know. Like I said, it was a long time ago. I think mommy might have sung that to me when I was growin' up. I remember a lot about those days now. We had lots of good times, but there were sad times, too. This generation wastes too much time worrying." She continued to swing slowly in the porch swing, its mournful creak blending with the hollering of the frogs in the valley below the house.

"If it's all the same to you all, I think I'll take a walk," said John L. with a significant look to Rob that he was to follow. "I've got to walk off that good supper. I ate a way too much."

As the two walked through the yard, they discussed whether to try to walk back to the Gap or wait on Johnny. "The day's gone anyway," said Rob. "We might as well wait on him. I don't want to have to come back tomorrow after the truck and him be gone again. We might as well try to get it out when we'll have some help. He'll be back directly."

It was dark now and the sun had set over Big Hill. Venus was shining like a diamond in a sapphire sky to the west and a grey band of clouds to the far east were all that remained of the afternoon storm.

"Must be dogwood winter comin' on," said Rob as a cool wind rustled the young leaves of the poplars.

"No doubt. It'll probably frost tomorrow night. "By the way, do you think that ballad she sang was about somebody in real life or it was made up?"

"Who knows," said Rob as they sat down on a wet sandstone ledge in the field behind the house.

"That talk about the red tree. I wonder if there's any connection with the one we saw today."

"I think your imagination has got the best of you, as usual, and I'm gonna go get that tree and plant it in yore yard if you don't hush about it." Rob sat and twisted the stick that he had whittled on back and forth as if this would cause it to assume a recognizable form that could be put to some use. After a while, he looked up. "Well, let's go."

"Go where?"

"Up to look at that tree. I know your dyin' to. See if Donna will loan you a light of some kind."

John L. was back in an instant, coal oil lantern in hand. Rob was already climbing the hill, sassafras stick between his teeth, headed for the cliff with the red tree below it. It was totally dark now except for a faint glow on the horizon that could be the remains of a sunset or the lights of Richmond. All was quiet but for the call of the whippoorwill and water dripping off the maple leaves and the oak twigs which were yet to be adorned.

"Have you ever seen a whippoorwill?" John L. asked.

"Mostly just heard 'em. I saw a great horned owl once. Had a six foot wingspread. Came right at me out of a laurel thicket and nearly scared me to death."

Another half hour of sloshing and climbing brought them to the Old State Road that they had left earlier in the day. Pretty soon John L. exclaimed, "I think that this is the swag in the road where that spring comes down from off that cliff."

"Then I reckon here's where we go up. Hold that light higher so I can see where I'm goin'.

They grabbed hold of one wet sapling after another sticking the toes of their boots into the side of Big Hill as they climbed toward the sandstone rockhouse. The yellow light of the lantern did little to dispel the shades of grey that colored the mountain since sunset. The dogwood blooms didn't seem as numerous and were beaten down by the afternoon rain.

"It's got to be here somewhere," said John L.

"I think it's somewhere close to this old windrooted tree," said Rob as he balanced himself on the wet bark of a fallen chestnut oak.

John L. held the lantern even higher. There it was. Just a few feet away. The blossoms, so pink earlier, were pale in the lantern light and probably would be gone in a day or two.

"Well, we're here. Now what?" queried Rob as he jumped off the log and took a seat on a pile of rocks.

For a minute, John stood stock still studying the situation. A million thoughts were running through his head. "You know, Rob, this time I think you're sitting on the answer."

Rob looked up quizzically. "These rocks?"

"Yep"

"These ain't nothin' but the corner of an old cornfield or somebody's attempt at one."

John kicked at the rocks. "I think there's something buried there."

"Naw."

"I'm sure of it. That's the only answer."

"You're gonna get copperhead bit as sure as I'm standin' here," said Rob as John began to dismantle the rock pile. "Well, I might as well get copperhead bit, too," Rob muttered as he began to help John.

Some of the rocks rolled down the hill hitting other ones with a hollow knock. Some landed with a dull thud in the wet leaves. After a couple of minutes, they uncovered a flat rock bigger than the others. It was limestone. A cut stone at that.

"What do you reckon's underneath it?" Rob asked apprehensively as they knelt down in the dim light to clear the leaves and dirt off the rock. "Don't reckon it's a grave, do ye?"

"No. I don't think so. And anyway, it won't hurt to lift the rock."

They scooted the rock to one side and in a small indentation under it surrounded by other flat stones was a small metal box. Rob carefully lifted it out and set it on the damp oak leaves. The two looked at each other in the dim lantern light as the cool wind whistled in the pine trees on the ridge. Rob got out his pocket knife, bent down and began prying on the edges of the box.

"Now, be careful. Something in there might break," said John as he too bent down to get a closer look, hardly daring to even guess what might be in the box.

After much prying and a little bending, the lid reluctantly opened. The light of the lantern revealed a rolled up sheaf of papers and a small leather pouch.

Rob took the papers and carefully untied the pink ribbon that had held them in place for so many years. The papers were yellowed with age and the edges almost disintegrated at the touch, but they were largely intact after what would prove to be over a century's patient waiting on this ridge.

John opened the brittle pouch and poured the contents into his hand. A two and a half dollar gold piece and a few silver quarters and dimes gleamed in the light. Also, there was a small twig. Anything that might have been attached to it was long gone.

"A pink dogwood blossom from a long time ago," thought John.

"What do those papers say?" John asked Rob as he moved closer so he could see them.

"Looks like to me they're goin's on that took place during the Civil War. They're all hand written and hard to read. But it doesn't say who wrote them. They don't have nobody's name on them. Looks like you made a better haul with the money in that pouch."

"Don't be so sure," said John as he once again poured the money out into his hand to look at it. This time a small folded piece of paper fell out. John carefully unfolded it and got near enough to the light to read it aloud.

My darling,

By now you have heard my song and
are on your way back to me. I was afraid
to bring these things with me for fear of
being robbed along the road. I can't stay
here in this holler and accept charity from
those who don't believe in freedom for all
as you and I do. If anything happens to me,
these tokens of my life and my love will be
here for you. I can trust no one these days.
Whatever happens, I know our love will
be for all time. In hopes of seeing you
soon.

Becky

Rob turned away from the letter and stood facing the darkness.

"What do you think about that?" asked John after taking a few seconds to catch his breath over the sheer wonderment of it all.

Rob said nothing.

"Well?"

"That's my people."

"What?"

"Becky Lainhart was Daddy's great-grandmaw."

Both men stood in silence for what seemed an eternity as the only sound was the drip of water off the trees and the rush of Cowbell Creek far below.

Rob spoke. "I told you that my great-great Grandfather was killed at Vicksburg. I guess that's why the box is still here."

"I wonder why Becky never came back for it?" asked John, still holding the letter.

"I don't know. I've heard my Grandpaw tell about his daddy being raised by Uncle Delmer's people. Maybe she died after she went back up Owsley Fork or maybe with the war and the children she just never got back here. Maybe she couldn't bear to come back here. I just don't know. Let's see that letter again."

Rob read the letter again and turned and looked up the holler.

John L. couldn't read his face.

Rob folded the letter and put it back in the box and turned to John and said, "I guess we'd better see if Johnny's got home yet."

An hours walk later, the lights from the windows of Lellie's old house appeared. Even though it was pitch dark now, Lellie was still sitting in the porch swing with a sweater wrapped around her shoulders.

Rob and John climbed the bowed steps once again. "Tell Johnny that we'll be back tomorrow and we'll need his help," said Rob.

Lellie smiled. "I'll tell him."

As they walked across the yard and up the narrow dirt road that led through the woods and eventually back to U.S. 421, John handed the box to Rob. "Your turn."

Lellie watched them until they disappeared from sight, a faint smile on her weathered face. She hummed a little of Rebecca's Lament and was lost in thought of things that happened in this holler long ago on starlit nights like this one.

A whippoorwill sounded in the distance. "Wonder what song he's singin'?" asked John L.

"I don't know," answered Rob. "I guess everybody's got to sing their own."

They walked on, box in hand, soft earth underfoot, just as Becky Lainhart had done so long ago.

REBECCA'S LAMENT

1. Do think it was Lellie's idea for Donna's family to live with her? Why or why not?

2. Imagine some of the hardships that were caused by family members being away from home for months or years at a time during the Civil War. Which of those hardships do or do not exist now when family members are in the armed services and are away from home for extended periods of time?

RESEARCH: Ask an older family member if there any ballads, songs or stories that have been handed down in your family.

RESEARCH: Did any of your ancestors serve in the Civil War? Were any of them involved in conflicts in other countries before your forebearers emigrated to America?

THE PALE ORCHID

John L. sat slumped in the seat of his truck and watched the waning moon set slowly over Big Hill. When it completed its trek over this wild country, there would be an hour of almost total darkness with the dim red Mars overhead and bright Venus to the west before the gray dawn brought the Deer Stables to life. A pair of headlights pulled off of U.S. 421.

"Dreaded Red," thought John. No doubt about it. He heard Ike's red '79 Chevy pickup slide to a stop in the gravel in front of Bret Rose's house.

Bret had seen the lights, too, for about that time he gently shut the front door to his house, walked across the yard and kicked the side of John's truck.

"Get out if you're goin'. It's late."

John opened the truck door, slowly got out, and took his shotgun and backpack over to Ike's truck. If this hadn't been a planned and long awaited venture, the three men wouldn't have recognized each other in their face masks.

Ike started the truck and headed toward Raccoon Creek. It was a silent trio, each with their own expectations of the day to come. The wind whistled around the tops of the truck doors, long minus their rubber seals and the muted call of a turkey box could be heard somewhere under the gear stowed in the truck floor. To hunt the wild turkey had been a ritual of spring and fall in these mountains for generations and today would be no exception, for the Horse Lick country was the ancestral homeland of more than one branch of each of their families.

"Don't forget we've got to pick up Bo," reminded John as the road narrowed and was now flanked by high banks and leafless sumac bushes, the victim of a clear-cut of times past.

"Do you think he'll be ready?" asked Ike.

"Don't know," answered John L. as he looked straight ahead and remembered his own first trip into these woods and what an impression it had made. Turkey hunting was serious business with Ike and Bret and he hoped he hadn't made a mistake in inviting a kid that had never hunted before.

"Don't worry. He'll do fine," said Bret. "After all he was born and raised out here."

Bret, the perpetual optimist, thought John L. He always looks at the good side of everything. I guess that's why his fifth graders like him so much.

John had taught Bo in the fourth grade five years ago and now had his little brother Perry in class. Bo had always been a quiet kid, but there was no mistaking an intelligence and subtle curiosity behind his black eyes. Bo's aunt Dorie picked them up after school and sometimes John would get a chance to talk to Bo while he and Dorie waited on Perry. Bo was a loner. He seemed to get his sustenance from nature. John remembered that he was always bringing a bug or rock to show him and that he could ask a million why's. He didn't know much about Bo's family except that where they lived was pretty isolated and that his parents never came around the school or showed up when he played on the grade school basketball team that Bret had coached. There was something unusual about him, though. Something about the way he reached out to his teachers but never knew exactly how to grasp what he was given.

John's thoughts of Bo assumed the form of reality as the headlights glanced off a lone figure walking toward them on the side of the road. He was clad in a long, green Army coat that only revealed a couple of inches of ragged jeans stuffed into black, tightly laced boots.

Ike stopped the truck in the middle of the road and John got out to greet his friend and former student. "Where's your gun?" asked John, momentarily alarmed that he had assumed that Bo's daddy or somebody in the family had one that they would loan him.

Bo pulled a scratched and weathered twelve gauge from underneath the coat and proudly held it with both hands. His eyes flashed with excitement and at that moment John knew that he had done right to ask him to come with them.

"Well, climb in the truck with us. We'll make room somewhere and don't put that gun back under your coat.

"Nope. I'll ride in the back," answered Bo, already vaulting himself into the truck bed that was normally only home to empty pop cans and an occasional coon dog.

"You sure?"

"Yep. Beats walkin'."

"Suit yourself," said John as he climbed back into the truck and they took off again for Raccoon.

Ike parked the truck at the edge of the creek near one of the Raccoon fords and everyone got out. It was still dark down in this holler even though the pale orchid of dawn was appearing through scattered clouds above the big oaks on the Boss Carpenter Ridge.

Ike lit his propane lantern and everyone began the last minute preparations for the big day ahead. Everyone except Bo. He watched silently as Bret put a camo sack on his shotgun and put on green mesh gloves so that he would hopefully be invisible to an unsuspecting turkey.

"Don't guess I need to do much to hide this gun," said Bo as he looked at the shotgun that he held in his hands. Its shine was long gone from many a rough trip from behind the seat of a pickup. Just the same he stuck his hand in the sandy, black earth on the bank above Raccoon Creek and rubbed some of it on the stock of the gun and some on his face like he had seen pictures in hunting magazines.

Within ten minutes, all was ready and Ike turned out the light and whispered to the others. "Bret and I'll go up the creek and set up in the next little holler. John, you and Bo head down toward Horse Lick. I believe there's a bench a little ways up on the bank not far from here. We'll meet back here at the truck in the late part of the mornin'. Luck to ye."

Bo followed John in silence trying hard not to slip and fall on the dry brown chestnut oak leaves that rested on slick black earth and were covered with a heavy frost that glistened in the rays of John's flashlight. The sound of footsteps and the rush of the creek seemed so loud in this land where each passing minute brought a little more light to quietly reveal the secrets of Raccoon.

"Here we are," said John as they set the gear down behind a tall, hollow red oak.

Bo watched John's every move as John got out a crow call, a turkey box and a slate.

"Wanna try it?" John whispered as he handed the crow call to Bo.

"What do you do with it?" asked Bo.

"You blow into it."

Bo blew into the hollow plastic tube and the loudness of it in the still woods made him jump. "Is that what a turkey sounds like?" he asked.

"No. That's what a crow sounds like. You've heard a crow before, haven't you?"

"Yeah."

"You see, a turkey will answer to the call of several different birds this time of year or sometimes just any kind of noise. It's mating season and they're real excited."

"Oh."

"Now here's how this slate works," said John, as he got out the round, flat disc and the plastic striker. He pushed down on the slate disc with the striker and with a quick snap of his wrist made a clucking sound that imitated a hen. "And you can make another kind of sound by just scraping the striker over the disc," he said as Bo watched. "Here, you try it."

Bo looked at John, not fully believing that he was actually getting a chance to do something he had only heard his daddy's friends talk about to this point. He took the slate and tried to imitate John's skilled movements.

"Hey, I think you could fool a turkey's own mama," said John. Bo glowed with a new confidence and enthusiasm. "Why don't you take that slate and go around the ridge a little ways and stake out a place for yourself."

"You mean it?" whispered Bo.

"Yeah, but keep hid. Somebody'll think you're a twenty pounder and you'll get shot, for sure."

The last that John saw of Bo was the back of his orange vest as it disappeared into the grey mist of the early morning. John was secretly glad that he would get a chance to relax a little and try his own skills.

A little before noon, John began walking back up the creek toward the truck. Bret and Ike were already there leaning against the tailgate.

"Where's yore turkey dinner?" asked Ike as he polished the stock on his Browning.

"The only thing I called up was a couple of crows and some of Tom Isaac's cows over on the next ridge. And besides the fact that I'm froze to death, it's been a pretty good mornin'."

"How was your luck?"

Ike grinned and glanced into the truck bed. "A sixteen pounder. Too bad it ain't Thanksgiving."

"You must have had that one scouted out."

"I dug enough 'sing in these woods last year to pay my truck insurance and sometimes I see turkey sign."

"I thought you were awful anxious to give directions this morning and like a fool I listened to you," John said.

"Where's your buddy?" asked Bret.

"He went on around the ridge. If he don't show up soon, I guess we'll have to go after him."

After speculation on who else might be lucky enough to kill a bird this season and the special secret techniques that Ike had used to kill his, the three got in Red and started back up Raccoon in the direction of where John had left Bo hours before.

"Let's park here and see if we see any sign of him," John said after they had driven as close as they could to where he thought Bo might be.

As they piled out of the truck, what sounded like a turkey in distress could be heard close by. Ike looked at the others and instinctively grabbed for his ten gauge. John held up his hand and said, "let's listen. That might be Bo. I gave him the slate."

"What?" asked Ike. I can't believe you. No wonder you didn't call up anything."

John didn't answer and began walking in the direction of the sound followed by the others. Soon, they spied Bo leaning against the light gray bark of an old beech tree. When he saw them he held his fingers to his lips as a signal to be quiet. The three stopped and listened as Bo put the turkey call down but didn't here anything except a squirrel cutting on some hickory nuts.

As they walked up to Bo, he said, "hear that."

"Hear what?" asked Bret.

"Listen!"

Ike, John and Bret all looked at each other and couldn't help but laugh. "That's a squirrel cuttin'," said Ike. "You've heard squirrels cut before, haven't you?"

"Yeah, I guess I have," said Bo as his face fell. "It sounded so much like this slate I thought for sure I had something."

"At least you called up a squirrel. That's more than I did," said John.

"Yeah. I guess it's time to go, huh?" asked Bo.

"'Bout time to head back to the Gap and get some sleep," said Ike.

Bo didn't have a word to say. It wasn't hard to see that he felt totally foolish, but nothing could be said to remedy the situation at this point.

"Did you stay in that one place all morning or did you move around a little?" asked John.

"I did go down to the creek for a little while."

"What did you get into there?" asked Bret, trying his best to make conversation.

"I saw some turkey tracks and I took pictures of them."

"With what?" asked John.

Bo dug into the coat pocket and dug out a 35mm camera that looked to be at least thirty years old. "Mommy got it for me at a yard sale for ten dollars."

"I'd say she got a real deal," said John, looking through the viewfinder and scratched lens that had specks of dirt on it. "A little cleaning and it'll be like a new one."

"I took some pictures of some flowers coming up down there, too," said Bo with a hint of excitement in his voice. "This is the first roll of film I've put in it. I hope it turns out." He paused. "I guess I ain't much of a hunter, am I?"

"I wouldn't say that," said Ike. "I've been ten years killing my first turkey. I wouldn't give up anytime soon."

Bo once again vaulted himself into the bed of the truck, this time his mood one of despair instead of anticipation. His long black curls blew in his face as he sat with his back against the truck cab on the trip toward home.

When Ike pulled up in front of Bo's house there was a man standing in the yard. He bore a resemblance to Bo except he was shorter and his hair was lighter. His mouth was set in a grim line and his eyes narrowed to a squint when he saw Bo get out of the back of the truck. Ike, Bret and John glanced in the direction of Bo's dad and realized there was going to be trouble.

"He looks drunk to me," said John. "Perry told me the other day that they hadn't seen him for a week."

"Too bad he's back," commented Ike.

As Bo walked down the bank to his house, the man walked toward him from behind, jerked the gun from Bo's hands and gave him a hard shove in the back that sent him stumbling toward the front porch. The camera fell out of his coat pocket, hit the ground and bounced a few feet along the rocky ground.

All three men saw what happened and stared in disbelief. Bret, who was sitting next to the passenger side door, jumped out of the truck, his fists clenched.

John was out of the truck in a split second and jumped in front of him. "Now's not the time," he said.

Bret's face was livid with rage. His blue eyes, usually the epitome of serenity were full of hatred and rage as he focused on Bo's dad. His gritted his teeth and his mouth was too dry to say a word as his mind flashed scenes from a time in his past when he was much, much younger. The mental image was more than real as he recalled his chin hitting the ground hard and being kicked across the yard. Now, he didn't even remember the crime, only the hate. And the hate was much easier to endure than the pain hidden deep in his spirit. As John coaxed Bret back into the truck, Ike got out of the driver's side and walked toward the house. He bent over and picked up the camera, as Bo's dad glared at him. Ike stood up and gave the man a look that said "pick on me and you'll be pickin' yourself up out of the dirt."

The trip back to the Gap was in total silence, but not for a lack of something to say. Many things would be said later when they were tempered with less emotion.

The following Monday, John didn't mention anything about the hunting trip to Perry, but watched him closely. Something was wrong. He had dark circles under his eyes and his face looked like it hadn't been washed for a day or two. When Dorie came to pick up Perry, John noticed that Bo wasn't with her. He walked a few steps behind Perry toward Dorie's '67 GTO. John had always liked that car. Even though it was beat and banged up and part of the hood had been painted with a brush, it was still a "goat." As she rolled down the window with one hand and pushed the glass down with the other, a cloud of cigarette smoke drifted skyward.

"Where's Bo?" he asked.

"That sorry daddy of his gave him a beatin'. That's where." That house is a bad place to be right now. I don't know why my sister stays with that man, if that's what you want to call him. Now, if he was mine, I'd..."

"Listen, Dorie," said John tersely. "Can you get a message to Bo without his family knowin' it?"

"Yeah, reckon I can."

"Tell him to meet me and Ike and Bret up at Ike's cabin tonight about dark. But tell him not to come if it'll cause trouble."

"Won't be no trouble. His old man is off and gone again and his mommy don't know where he goes and likely don't care."

"I'm counting on you, Dorie." She smiled and flipped the cigarette out the window.

"Consider it done." The old Pontiac roared off through the parking leaving a trail of blue smoke, one of it's tailpipes almost dragging the pavement. Perry looked wide-eyed at John through the rear window, his hand clutching one of his homework papers.

That night, John sat in a straight backed chair on the porch of Ike's cabin. He could hear Ike and Bret talking inside as they sat in front of the iron cook stove, orange firelight peeping through the cracks in its seams casting a glow on the rough wooden floor. The cabin was a hiding place from the routine of the world on spring and fall nights. John had told the others what had happened to Bo. They weren't surprised, but it was John who shouldered the blame because he had been the one who had asked Bo on the trip.

Directly, footsteps could be heard coming through the leaves that had been blown across the dirt road by the spring wind of the afternoon. It was Bo. He approached with his head ducked.

"Hey," greeted John as he got up from the chair. "Come on in. We've got a surprise for you."

Bo nodded without looking at John and stepped into the cabin. "How's our huntin' buddy," asked Ike as he got up and lit a propane lantern. In its glow, they saw that Bo's eye was swollen and the right side of his face, bruised. Even though the sight made John want to turn the other way, he look at him, grinned and said, "that's a nice 'un" as he examined his eye a little closer. Bo still didn't speak. He was not the same young man that had looked forward to his first turkey hunt. He was pale and looked half-starved.

"You look like you're hungry to me," said Ike, "and we've got some turkey fixed and deermeat, too. You've got to have some of it with us for bringin' luck to the hunt."

Bret handed him a plate full of meat and potatoes that had been fried with lots of onions in the black iron skillet.

"Yessir, Bo will be a real hunter when he gets a little age on him and a few more trips with us," said Ike.

Bo finally spoke up. "It's alright. I ain't as dumb as I look. You don't have to ever take me again."

"No, we don't," said Ike, "but we want to. Why, John here'll be thirty soon and we've got to train the younger generation."

"And we've got something else for you, too," said John. He held out a package of pictures that he'd had developed special that day at the newspaper office.

Bo looked up and took the package, his grimy hands opening it carefully as if it would break. He looked at the pictures and then looked back at John. Bo's eyes glistened as he managed a half smile. "Are these the pictures that I took?"

"Yep," Ike said as they all looked over Bo's shoulder. "And what's more," said John, "that white flower that you took a picture of is a Kentucky Lady's Slipper. They're really rare. I talked to the guys in Frankfort this afternoon and that's the first one ever found in this county. So there."

Bo looked at the pictures over and over and finally handed them to John, who looked at him and said, "they're yours - to keep."

Bo tucked the envelope carefully into the pocket of his long green coat and went out on the cabin porch and leaned against one of the rough locust posts that held it up. He listened to the frogs holler in the valley. They didn't seem a sound of the long dark night anymore. For this one instant in time, he was happy. The pain in his soul seem to vanish and his very being was warmed. Even he, who had known so little of the good in life knew enough to cherish this moment, for times like these might not come again soon.

John, Bret and Ike glanced through the open cabin door and watched Bo as he stood silently looking into the night. Bret didn't have to wonder what Bo was thinking. He was pretty sure that he knew and somehow the pain in his own heart eased a little.

"If you don't get in here, you're gonna miss a recap of Ike's big turkey story, not they we haven't heard it before," said Bret.

Bo turned and walked to the cabin door and stood there silhouetted in the light. He grinned. "I'm listenin'."

THE PALE ORCHID

1. Is hunting allowed in areas near your home? How do you feel about killing wild animals? Do you feel it is different than killing domestic animals for food (cows, chickens,etc.)?

2. Do you feel that endangered rare species like the Kentucky Ladyslipper should be protected? Why?

3. Could John L., Ike and Bret have done other things to make Bo feel good about himself and the environment in which he lived? What might they have done?

4. Do you think that Bo has a chance to better himself in life? How might he do this?

5. What are the major social problems in the area where you live that lead to physical abuse of children as well as adults?

RESEARCH: Contact the state government natural resources agency in your state to see if there are endangered species in your county. (Kentucky State Nature Preserves Commission in Kentucky) Ask how you might help to protect these species.

THE LEGEND OF BLUE FISH

"Missions, that's what we're all about. Always have been," said Layne Johnson.

Old Mrs. Martin nodded her head in fervent agreement. "We're all just pore folk, but that don't mean there ain't some worse off 'n us. Fact is, most of the souls in this world are pore, and hungry too. And we ain't hungry."

John L. slumped in his seat and looked from person to person as the debate continued whether White Oak Creek Church would send somebody this year to represent the congregation at the Elkhorn, North Carolina, mission meeting. He prepared for Aunt Lucy Carpenter's perennial tale of how her Poppa had journeyed into the hills of North Carolina in the early 1900's and found the need for spiritual guidance and social welfare even greater there than among his own kin.

"All the folks there were part Cherokee 'by pride or by birth,' Poppa would say." Aunt Lucy beamed at getting to tell her story to a couple of new members of the church board. Even though they knew the story well, they hadn't "officially" heard it. After Poppa had come back to Kentucky, the church had started a permanent fund to help the folks at Elkhorn build a school. A close bond had existed between the Elkhorn community and the White Oak Church to this day. Especially after Joe Turner's girl, Emmy, had gone down there as representative and married one of the Elkhorn boys.

The Elkhorn school had long since closed with the advent of consolidation. Now, the old building was used for a Community Action Center to help teach people to read, for GED training and making use of the talents of older adults as a means of providing them fulfillment as well as providing help to the community.

Aunt Lucy rambled on and on and ended her story with a motion that Alice Gaines be the delegate this year. Alice stood up and twisted her hands nervously and her face reddened, "I'd like to, but I've got to help my daughter-in-law put up corn. I don't want to have to feed her bunch all winter," she said with her annoying nervous laugh. "I decline."

"Just as well," thought John L. "She wouldn't make a good delegate. She'd never speak up. A good woman, but never had a thought of her own, I'd say."

"How about you, John?" asked Aunt Lucy. "You're new on the board. It'd be good for you, and you're a teacher and can write us up a big fine report. Won't be no trouble for you to do that. All for John L. goin', raise their hand." Everybody did.

John L. shrugged and half grinned. "I guess I can. I'll have to see."

Layne Johnson adjourned the meeting and everybody patted John L. on the back and told him what a fine delegate he would be. It was just over two weeks later that John L. headed over Laurel Fork on a foggy August morning for the mountains of North Carolina. The sun was rising over the mountains to the east of the RECC farm as John L.'s truck parted the fog on the ridge as he headed toward the interstate at London on his mountain journey. He grinned as he recalled what Aunt Lucy had said. "Cherokee, by pride or by birth." We'll see if things have changed since Poppa's day. About noon, John L. left the interstate and turned onto one crooked road after another, each of which climbed higher into the mountains outside Asheville. Finally, he reached Elkhorn. It wasn't like mountain towns in Kentucky in that it was located on a ridge, not a creek bottom. Even so, the ridge was dwarfed by the Smokies on the far distant horizon.

The old Elkhorn school was at the end of the town's only street. It was a clapboard structure that stood a couple of feet off the ground on columns made of cut stone. 1910 was carved on one of them. "Well, I'm here," John L. said to himself as he parked under one of two white oaks that graced the old school yard.

A woman sat on the steps and watched two little boys rassle in the dirt, each alternately yelling in victory over the other. John L. thought that the she looked vaguely familiar. As he approached her, she smiled and stuck out her hand. "I'm Emily O'Bryan. You know, Emmy Turner; Joe's girl."

"Glad to meet you," greeted John L. "I never thought of seein' you right off."

"Mommy called and said you were comin'. You're stayin' with us."

"I wouldn't want to put you out. I'll just check into a motel somewhere."

"Do you see any motels?" she grinned.

"Well, no, but I passed one....."

"Then, it's settled. We'll go to the house and get us something to eat before these young'uns kill one another. Mind if we take your ride? I walked."

"It's all yours," John L. motioned. He shook his head, feeling somewhat overwhelmed.

"Boys, get in," she yelled as they took off for John's truck. Emmy O'Bryan's rambling, white frame house was not but a quarter of a mile from the old school. It set upon a little knoll a good distance back from the street and was surrounded on three sides by a porch. The boys jumped out of the truck when it came to a stop and ran through the yard to see if their dad was home.

"Carter promised to take 'em fishin', but I'll tell you he's not home. Huntin' for work. He got laid off two months ago. He's an accountant and a good one, too. It's hard times here, John. I teach, you know, and that's pretty steady employment once you're tenured and I got that last year or I'd be out of a job, too, prob'ly."

"Why's that?"

"Oh, it's a long story and not a nice one either."

The boys bounded out the screen door about that time, slamming it shut. They alternately begged their mom to let them go fishing by themselves.

"No, boys. It's too dangerous down in that Dark Holler; snakes as big as your leg. Maybe bears, too." They eyed John L.

"I'll take 'em, Emmy. Right after lunch, guys. O.K.?"

The boys jumped off the porch in search of earthworms under the bricks surrounding the flowerbed around the porch.

Later that afternoon as John L. sat on the bank of Ashokan Creek watching the boys fish, he understood why this place was called the Dark Holler. Giant hemlocks grew in the spaces between moss covered boulders along the creek. The hillside was a solid tangle of rhododendron and mountain laurel. Even on a sunny August afternoon, it was cool here and every now and then a wave of even cooler air swept down from some cave in the hillside.

His thoughts of the primeval were interrupted by the bickering of the brothers. "You gotta put that one back," yelled the oldest of Emmy's boys to his little brother.

"I don't wanna. It's a big one."

"Granny says the blue fish are special. Throw it back or I'll tell." The smaller boy threw his catch back, throwing hateful glances at his brother and wistfully eyeing the fish as it disappeared under a rock in the water.

"Hmm," thought John L. to himself," wonder what's so special about the blue fish."

The boys caught a half a dozen more but the heat of the afternoon thwarted their efforts and pretty soon they were anxious to get back to the house to show off their fish. "Granny," they both yelled when they got in sight of home, "look what we caught."

A white haired woman sat in the porch swing. "I'll reckon you've caught your supper. You've got to clean 'em though. Here, take my knife." They disappeared around the corner of the house to the back porch where messes wouldn't be noticed.

"I'm Daisy O'Bryan; Emmy's mother-in-law," the woman announced as she got up. "I know. You're John L. Glad to meet you."

"I've heard a lot about you. The boys say you're the fish expert around here."

"I've caught a few in my time. Too old for that now."

"Well, I know why the boys like to go to the Dark Holler. It's twenty degrees cooler down there than it is here." John L. looked down the other side of the ridge that obviously split the two watersheds. "Aren't there any fish down there in that creek?" The stream was similar to the one in the Dark Holler in that it was strewn with large rocks it, but the hills heading down to it were treeless and covered with blackberry briars, Joe-Pye weed and black-eyed susans. The bases of the white boulders were cooled by water that flowed from mountaintops and hollers miles away from where Daisy and John sat.

"You'd better get a good look at Logan Creek down there. Hit'll be your last one if that Bannin man has his way." Daisy's words were like thunder in his ears compared to the faint rush of the water two hundred yards below.

"What?"

"That's what the meeting is about tonight at the school. I guess we'll be spendin' some time in board meetings together. I've been on it for years. You see, the church still owns four hundred acres that the school sets on. The land was used for an orchard and for farming a long time ago. There was a dormitory where the kids boarded. The students raised their own food and the school taught farming methods."

"What's that got to do with...."

"I'm a tellin' ye. Ed Bannin wants to have a lake built up here. A big lake. Says it will attract all kinds of tourists and help the economy. It'll help his economy alright. Word is that he's going to build a marina and it'll be just like always. Bannin gets richer and everyone else eats beans and mill gravy."

John looked confused. "So, what's that got to do with the school?"

"The church owns the school and that's one of the pieces of land that he has to have for access to the lake and of course he wants his big city backers to think he has community support and all of that kind of thing. We'll vote tonight on whether or not to sell the land."

"And I guess that you'll vote no."

"Right you are. Those Bannins came here right after the Civil War. I used to hear my daddy talk about them fencing off our mountains so the hogs couldn't roam. They were from up north. Bought several thousand acres here on the mountain and made a fortune in timber when the rest of us were burning dead limbs just to heat the house. Seems like every generation they all go off to make their fortune and the one that comes back knows it all and tears up our hills one way or another. Just when the timber over there across the mountain on Buckeye got big enough to be purty again, Ed's daddy mined the coal. Hit'll never be the same. Ain't nobody had good water since."

"How about Logan Creek?" John asked. "Is it poisoned, too?"

"It ain't the cleanest in the world, but the mine bench is on the other side of the mountain and that yeller water goes into Buckeye. I wouldn't even wade in Buckeye. Yep. The Bannins cut the trees, took the coal and now they're gonna cover it all up with water if they can. Yes sir. None of those Tennessee lakes for the Bannins. They want one over here and they'll get it, too. Everybody around here but a few thinks if a lake is built that they'll get rich themselves. Only the rich get richer, John. Well, we'd better get some dinner. My beans is prob'ly burnt by now. Check on the young'uns and their fish if ye would."

After supper, John L. waited on the front porch for Daisy so they could walk to the meeting together. As they walked down the street, he tried to visualize the valley with a lake, and the roar of jet boats as compared to the drone of the locusts that he heard now. He noticed that Daisy O'Bryan did not look at the valley as they walked down the street. She merely looked straight ahead as the west wind pushed her from behind and the setting sun glinted off her white hair. "A woman with a mission," John L. thought as he saw her black eyes riveted on a fat man standing on the schoolhouse steps. She walked more determinedly but not faster.

"Ed Bannin," thought John L. "It has to be."

A black Mercedes, keeping its distance from the doors of dusty Ford pickups and Chevettes, was parked on the roots of one of the oak trees in the schoolyard. Daisy walked by the black car and set her handbag on it with a clunk. "Can't seem to find my reading glasses, John." After much searching she gave up the hunt, strapped the purse over her shoulder and the two sauntered over to the school.

Ed Bannin had watched the whole scene. "Who's your buddy, Daisy?" Bannin asked as he stuck out his hand to John and patted Daisy on the back with the other.

"My name's John. Don't believe we've met."

"Ed Bannin," the big man said with a well practiced and equally insincere smile.

John and Daisy walked in to the meeting room with its straight backed chairs and long tables. As the meeting was called to order, John L. noticed that there were two men seated to Ed Bannin's right that seem to take all their cues from him. John glanced at each of the board members wondering how they would vote and what the outcome would be. Finally, after an endless number of trivial motions, the topic of the sale of the land for the lake came about.

"We all know Mr. Bannin," said Ella Talland, the board chairwoman, as she beamed up at Ed, "I'm sure we'll all be excited about the news he has for us."

Ed Bannin stood, cleared his throat pompously, and addressed the group. "You have in front of you a proposal that I'm sure all of you have read and studied with great care."

"What?" thought John as he glanced up sharply at Ed Bannin. "I've never seen this before in my life."

"We all know that the economy and quality of life in Elkhorn will be dramatically enhanced if this lake is built and for this reason I have availed myself to various persons to see that we in these mountains aren't overlooked. These gentlemen seated to my right are here to conduct some follow-up studies if our vote tonight is for the progress of our community."

After several minutes of discussion, John L. asked "What about the marina? Who will run it?"

Ed Bannin flashed his broadest smile. "Oh, that's a year or two down the road. It will mean more local jobs. I guarantee that."

Several nodded and smiled. John L. did not and Daisy had glared at Ed Bannin with a hardened stare since he had begun his presentation. A few others listened with interest but hadn't said much. Finally, the vote was taken by secret ballot. Everyone sat quietly while Daisy and Ella counted the votes. After what seemed an eternity, Ella announced "the vote is ten to four and Elkhorn can look forward to a bright future."

The meeting was adjourned and everyone gathered around Ed Bannin to talk about the new lake. Daisy got up slowly and walked toward the door. John L. followed close behind. As they walked back home in the darkness, the moon, almost full and rising behind them, was bright enough to make their shadows against the pavement.

Daisy was quiet for awhile, but then she said, "I knew they'd go for it. The Bannins always win."

A warm breeze brought the soft rush of water from Logan Creek from way down in the valley that was to their north. John L. looked in that direction as if to take it all in on his first and last night on Elkhorn ridge. He knew the days of the sound of the rushing water were numbered and wondered how many seasons it would be until the moon would reflect off a growing pool of dark water bounded by a wall of earth and rock. John didn't like dark water. It gave him cold chills just to think about it. He imagined that he could see the glint of the light off the ripples in Logan Creek and it sparked an idea in his mind that left him so lost in thought that he almost missed the sidewalk that led to Daisy's house.

The wind began to pick up a little as John and Daisy each took a chair on the front porch. "You know, my daddy told me things about that creek," Daisy said as she sat down. I hadn't thought about them for a long time until tonight. The story goes that when our people were forced from here a hundred and fifty years ago..."

"Our people?" asked John L.

"The Cherokee," Daisy answered softly; her black eyes reflecting sheets of distant lightning that were illuminating the northern sky with increasing frequency.

"Go on."

"Legend has it that there were fish that lived in Logan Creek that were special to the Cherokee. When the sun shined on them, they were as bright as gold. Daddy said there was lots of them right down there in that shoal that you can see from our house.

When the Cherokee went away, the fish were sad and all disappeared never to be seen again." She paused for a minute. "You know," Daisy said sarcastically, "I'll bet the fish really were sad because that's when people like the Bannins moved in and killed Logan Creek. If the creek were given a chance, it just might recover."

"What about the Dark Holler? Why is it still green?"

"That's my land," said Daisy, "and it'll stay green as long as I have anything to do with it. Daddy gave me that holler. We were dirt pore, but he wouldn't never sell it. Old man Bannin offered him a small fortune for it, but nothin' doin'. Carter feels the same way. Hit's in the blood."

"I'd say you've done nature a favor, Daisy. What about the blue fish the boys were talkin' about."

"That's another story."

"I'm, listenin'."

"Like I said, most of the Cherokee were herded out of here like cattle, including my ancestors. The second night away from here, my great-great Grandfather escaped and came back. He was just a boy. His parents figgered he would fare better by himself in the woods than wherever they were goin'. He hid out over in the high mountains above the Dark

Holler and set traps and fished at night. He told my Grandfather that if it hadn't been for the blue fish he would have starved to death. Folks have told me that the blue fish are endangered or something like that. I'm particular about who fishes there and what they catch. Anyway, my great-great Grandfather took the name Blue Fish. He also told my Granddaddy that he sold medicine to the folks around here. You know, herbs and things like that. I guess if it hadn't been for that, they probably would have run him off. Doctors was real scarce back then and he knew his plants and what they could cyore. Had to, just to live, I guess. He was awfully good with his hands, too, or least that's what I've been told. They was a man who was an old time blacksmith that lived around here at that time and he sort of took Blue Fish in and taught him the trade. That's how we got the Dark Holler. That man's widder gave it to him. She never had any childern and Blue Fish had helped them keep the place up. A lot of folks didn't like that much, but that's the way it happened. My daddy was a blacksmith, too. People came from everywhere to get him to make things. He could make harness, even shoes out of leather. We might have been pore, but the young'uns and the horses always had shoes." She laughed and shook her head. "Them was hard times, John."

Daisy paused and leaned back in her chair. The rumble of thunder could now be heard echoing across the valley. "Yessir, we'll get a storm tonight. You know John, my daddy would sit out on this porch after everybody had gone to bed and you know what he'd do? Make knives. He'd make 'em out of saw blades. Saws was made out of real metal back then. I'd watch out the window at him a settin' out here with a coal oil lamp and he'd work a way into the night. He could have sold 'em for big money. But no. He gave 'em away. Mommy would get real mad about it sometimes. But he'd just laugh and say they was things money couldn't buy."

The wind was blowing hard enough now to rattle the extra chain hanging from the top of the porch swing. "Yep, John, a lot's happened on this ridge. Those Bannins have kept things tore up since the day they set foot here and now they are gonna lay the place to rest once and for all by a coverin' it with water. Makes me sick. I'd as soon dangle my feet in one of those deep holes in the creek as a whole lake full of water. I'd rather my Grandyoung'uns fish off a rock with a cane pole than off of somebody's big boat and them a drinkin' and carryin' on. That's what it's comin' to, though.

Progress, they say. I call it by a different name and I'm glad to do it. Well, I've talked yer leg off, but what's done is done and I'm goin' to bed. More meetings in the morning. On community education, I think." Daisy laughed. "I'm surprised any of the folks around here think they need any education. They're so smart." The screen door slammed and Daisy disappeared into the house.

John L. leaned back in his chair and watched the black shadows of the maple limbs move to and fro against the yard, lit up by the moon, now high in the sky, as bright as silver, and casting a pale, bluish light on the grass. In a few minutes it would be covered by the clouds scudding quietly from the north.

The thunder was closer, now. John counted the seconds between lightning's flash and thunder's roar. Four miles, then three. He looked down and saw Daisy's beans drying on a sheet on the porch floor. He picked them up, took them in the house and then came back out, the sheet draped over his arm and disappeared toward the Dark Holler.

The next morning, John L. was awakened at seven by Emmy's knock on his bedroom door. "You've got work to do. Meetings. Are you gonna sleep all day?" she yelled through the door.

John looked at his wet clothes that hung over the closet door and dragged himself out of bed, too tired to be anxious about what the day would hold. At a little after nine, he and Daisy arrived at the old school. The same faces were there as the night before, all of them more rested than John's and brighter than Daisy's.

The morning session was fairly uneventful and Ella Talland called the meeting to order again after lunch. About 2:30, Ed Bannin's two consultants walked in and took their seats. Ed smiled at them and then focused his attention on Ella. He radiated with an aura of triumph as she introduced him again. "I'll turn the meeting over to our two friends who have been doing some studies on our mountain," Ella said. "I'm sure they'll have good news for us."

One of the men stood and started to read from his notebook and then seemed to change his mind. He put the notebook down, paused, and began to speak. "My colleague and I have found something very interesting just this morning that other studies seemed to have missed. In short, Logan Creek is home to an endangered species of fish and even though much study has been done as far as environmental impact is concerned, a lot more will have to be done.

"How long will that take?" Ella asked.

"We just don't know. It make take months or even years," the consultant answered.

"Does that mean the lake won't be built?" asked one of the board members.

"Only time will tell," Bannin's henchman answered. "All we know right now is that a lot of further study will have to be done."

Daisy looked at John, not knowing what to say. John was trying to look as shocked as the others.

Ed Bannin's face was contorted with rage as he looked at the consultant, "You're not going to let some stupid fish stop my ... uh, our lake."

"Well, Mr. Bannin, that.."

"That, nothing. We'll see about this," said Ed Bannin as he turned and left the room.

Ella adjourned the meeting for a ten minute break. John and Daisy walked out onto the porch as the black Mercedes disappeared rapidly in a cloud of dust, even though Elkhorn's main street wasn't long enough for it to get past second gear.

"Well, well," said Daisy to herself as she looked in the direction of Logan Creek.

John L. knew that even though she couldn't see the water, she was there in spirit.

"John, let's go see those fish. I can't sit another minute." Daisy was already off the porch and had headed toward a narrow path through the tall grass that led to Logan Creek. By the time they reached the water, which was flowing swiftly after the previous nights rain, both of them were muddy and wet from the knees down.

"John, I don't see any fish; just some minners."

"Let's look down here in some of these deep holes," said John as he twirled a foxtail stalk between his fingers and ambled on down the creek.

Daisy looked at him quizzically and asked, "How did you know there was deep holes down there?"

"Oh, just figgered."

The cold front had moved through and the clouds were riding on a cool northwest wind as they cast giant moving shadows on the mountains.

"There's a fish," said Daisy excitedly, "and it's a blue fish too." She paused for a minute. "John, did you have anything to do with this?"

He shot her his most innocent look and just grinned. About that time, a patch of sunlight crossed Logan Creek, flooding water and rocks with color. For a few seconds, John and Daisy stood motionless, staring into the water. The blue fish glinted of pure gold in the sun as they flitted through the ripples and darted under rocks.

"I don't guess a ray of sun has ever struck the Dark Holler. This is something new for them," said John, not immediately realizing what he had just revealed.

They stood and watched the fish for a long time, each of them hoping that this would be a pleasure that could be one day taken for granted.

Later, as they walked back up the hill, Daisy stopped and reached into the side pocket of her purse, pulled out a small pocketknife and placed it in John's hand. The handle was stained blue and had a fish carved in it.

"It was daddy's," said Daisy. "He would want you to have it."

"No, I can't take.."

"Yes, you will, and that's that."

After holding it motionless for a few seconds, John slowly looked up at Daisy and said, "it's beautiful." He could say no more. As John L. walked, the knife still in his hand, he couldn't seem to get enough of the bright, blue late summer sky, the white clouds, the purple of the ironweed, and the red of the cardinal flower. He dodged the little sassafras and pine seedlings, a year old, coming up through the fescue and imagined this place two centuries ago and maybe a century from now. He held the knife in front of him and turned it one way and then the other so the blade would catch the rays of the afternoon sun. He thought now of home and the story he wouldn't tell when he returned. "Cherokee, by pride or by birth," he thought. Maybe things haven't changed much at all since Poppa's day.

Daisy led the way as John walked on toward Elkhorn, the music of Logan Creek behind him and in his heart the proud spirit of the people who loved and nurtured this land long ago and to this day.

THE LEGEND OF BLUE FISH

1. What do think is meant by the term "Cherokee, by pride or by birth?"

2. Do you think the proposed dam would bring prosperity to the area? What are some of the things that might be lost if the dam is built? What might be gained?

3. Why do you think that Emmy Turner stated that she might lose her job if she did not have tenure with the school system?

4. Do you think that those who mine minerals on their own land have the right to cause to cause water quality problems downstream? What solution do you propose to this dilema?

5. The story only implies that John moved the fish from one stream to the other. Do you think he would have been justified in doing this? Why or why not?

6. Why do you think some people have a close association and respect for the land and others do not?

7. If you had been against the dam being built, how would you have gone about stopping it or would you have said or done anything at all?

RESEARCH: What was the Trail of Tears? Why did it occur? Are there similar events that have happened in America in the twentieth century? Are there groups of people in you community that are discriminated against and forced to live a lifestyle that is not of their choice?